The Spirit Collector

HAZEL WATSON MYSTERY BOOK FIVE

C.A. VARIAN

Copyright © 2023 by C.A. Varian

All rights reserved.

No part of this publication may be reproduced, distributed, or transmitted in any form or by any means, including photocopying, recording, or other electronic or mechanical methods, without the prior written permission of the publisher, except as permitted by U.S. copyright law. For permission requests, contact C.A. Varian @ https://cavarian.com/

The story, all names, characters, and incidents portrayed in this production are fictitious. No identification with actual persons (living or deceased), places, buildings, and products are intended or should be inferred.

Book Cover by Leigh Cadiente Designs

Contents

Dedication	V
Prologue	3
The Warning	
1. Collector of Souls	13
2. The Missing Spirits & The Missing Girl	25
3. The Salt Line	37
4. Gone Without a Trace	47
5. Return to the Swamp	55
6. Congratulations	65
7. Sharing the News	75
8. The Void	85
9. An Ordinary Girl with Extraordinary Visions	95
10. The Ghostly Underworld	103
11. The Crone, The Spirit, & The Raven	111
12. A Little R & R	123

13.	Friends and Allies	135
14.	Returning to the Void	149
15.	Venturing Into the Murky Water	159
16.	Beacon of Hope in the Darkness	171
17.	Crossing Into the Light	185
18.	Hope for the Future	193

Epilogue	201
The Darkness that Follows	
Enjoyed The Spirit Collector?	205
Also By C.A. Varian	206
Follow C.A. Varian	208
About the Author	209

In memory of my dad, who passed away on August 1, 2023

I love and miss you. We all do.

Cherie

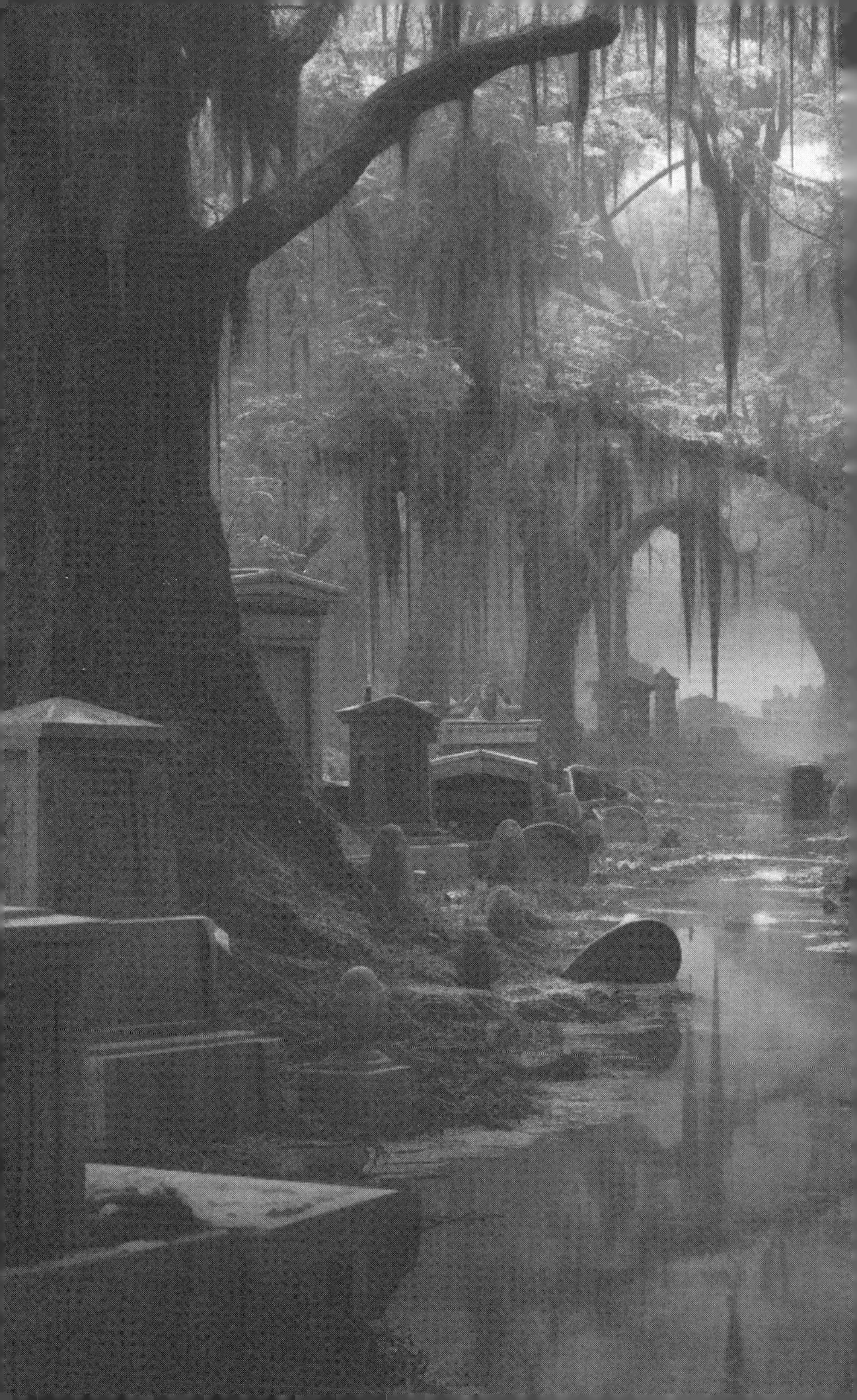

Prologue

The Warning

"A passenger plane went down near Holy Ghost Campground an hour ago."

Time stood still as Hazel stared at the screen of her phone, at the ominous message her mother had sent her. She didn't even know why her mother was awake at such an hour, but Sandi had abilities similar to her own, so it was possible her mother had been woken by something innate, some supernatural force telling her that souls somewhere needed help.

Tate took charge when Hazel couldn't, responding to her mother before grabbing his own phone to message the detective. They hadn't heard back from Detective Bourgeois since his last message, but neither of them was surprised. Everything had happened too quickly for anyone to prevent the crash. She knew that in her mind, even if some part of her hated herself for not stopping it from happening.

Leaving their phones on the bed near them, Tate pulled her against his chest, tipping her head back so her eyes met his. "This isn't your fault. Do you hear me? You couldn't have prevented this."

She heard him, but the words didn't quite register. Whether or not she could have prevented the crash, there was nothing she could do now that the incident had already happened. Well, nothing aside from helping any spirits who hadn't crossed through to where they belonged, or to wherever the black mass would take them. The thought of the mysterious entity luring the dead anywhere unsettled her, but what could she do about it? With the investigation and cleanup at the crash site, she wouldn't be able to go to the scene for weeks, possibly longer. She truly was helpless.

Blinking rapidly, Hazel tried to pull herself into the present, the present with Tate, and not the present that was happening miles away. "I'm trying to accept that. It just may take a while."

Tate nodded and kissed her forehead, the warmth of his lips lingering. "Just know how much I love you, and I understand." Her body warmed as he leaned in to kiss her lips. "Just know that there's nothing we can do about any of this. My plans haven't changed. I'm still taking you home."

Allowing him to pull her into his chest, she closed her eyes, the exhaustion of the past days draining her energy and leaving behind the shell of someone too tired to fight. Sleep took her before she had a chance to think about anything else.

The next morning was flooded with news of the crash, although the authorities were still trying to figure out what had caused it. Sixty-seven souls were on that plane, and not one survived.

The grief was a physical entity, sitting like a black cloud next to Hazel all morning. Tate looked after her, fussing over her like he had after she'd been rescued from Raymond Waters' cabin of horrors in the Louisiana swamp. She let him. She didn't have any energy to take care of herself, anyway.

They left the hotel as soon as they woke, grabbing breakfast and coffee from a drive thru, before heading toward her parents' ranch. The food tasted like sawdust in her mouth, but she forced herself to chew and swallow, a robotic function meant to keep her from vomiting all over the car. She didn't know how much she had to lose, but she figured her stomach could dig something up if given the chance.

Candy and Jake returned to them that morning, both horrified at the developments. As Hazel suspected, the pair had returned to the hotel once she and Tate drove away from the crossroads. Candy admitted to peeking into their hotel room hours later, but they'd both been asleep by that point, so she didn't bother them.

The offer stood open for them to stay the night at her parents' home, but Hazel had no interest in doing so. Tate admitted the same. Any minute they stayed in Santa Fe that day was a minute too long. So, after a brief lunch with her parents, they left for their sixteen-hour drive back to Louisiana. Sure, they'd have to stop overnight, and the rental car would cost a fortune when they left it in a new location, but it didn't matter. Although Hazel realized flying truly was a safe way to travel, she couldn't bring herself to do it. At least not yet.

They traveled for a while before stopping in a rural Texas town that Hazel couldn't name. They trudged into their hotel room, showered, and fell asleep as soon as their heads hit the pillows. She was so exhausted that the entire ordeal had been a blur. Her mother updated her on news about the crash, but there had still been no update on the cause. With the ongoing investigation, it was unlikely the authorities would make those details public after only one day. The cause didn't matter, anyway, at least not to Hazel. No matter why the plane had crashed, she'd failed those people, even if she had been powerless to stop it.

Waking up the following morning, she was surprised to have not been haunted by any nightmares or visits from Bella. It was possible that the crash had ended those particular communications, but she didn't want to place any bets on it. Her interactions with the spirit world had rarely ever gone as planned, but she was glad to have gotten a semi-restful night of sleep, no matter what the reasoning for their silence was.

When she and Tate left the hotel room for the last leg of their journey to New Orleans, they were both beyond tired of being away from home. Candy and Jake had popped up in the backseat halfway to Austin, bringing a bit of entertainment as Candy sang along–very loudly–to the radio. Candy truly was an entertaining woman, even after death. Things rarely seemed to bother her, and if they did, she didn't let it show.

Knowing that Hazel was in a difficult place, no one tried to fool her into thinking otherwise. They were simply supportive, which she appreciated. Tate and Candy were exactly who she needed in her life and Jake was always a neutral party, which she appreciated all the same.

A collective breath left them when they crossed the Luling Bridge, which brought them close to their neighborhood. Candy and Jake had faded out somewhere around Baton Rouge, tired of the drive and having no reason to withstand it. Unfortunately for Hazel and Tate, they had no choice but to keep trucking along.

It was a surreal experience for her to return to their home as a married woman, a home that hadn't been hers for very long but seemed like it had been forever. Her relationship with Tate had been a whirlwind romance, a friendship that blossomed over seven years to become something that would last forever. Even with her obligation to the spirits she knew would inevitably find her later, there was no place she would have rather been than in their home. When she laid in bed that night, she did so wrapped in the arms of a man who would withstand any storm with her, and would put his foot down when the winds became too dangerous.

The sound of the television came into focus, and the smell of her mother's vanilla candle made its way to her nose before Hazel could see the visual of where she was. She walked through her parents' ranch home, not knowing where she was going, but simply following the signs of life. She wasn't sure why she was seeing the home. She and Tate had been back in New Orleans for a week, settling into their lives as a married couple, which hadn't changed their lives much at all.

There was a familiar pundit on the television, making claims about things he had no knowledge of, seeking to influence the public. She and Tate didn't watch the program, but she was still familiar with it. Stepping forward as though she was moving with a purpose, Hazel entered the den.

Darkened by night, the only light in the room came from the television. Her mother was nowhere in sight, but her father was sitting on the sofa, remote in hand and a sleepy look on his face.

Hazel didn't even attempt to speak to him, because she knew he wouldn't be able to hear her. Like so many times before, she knew she wasn't really there. Instead, Hazel sat on the chair opposite her father and watched him. Aside from the hospital and the brief visit after he'd been discharged, she hadn't been in the same room with her father in five years. Even if he couldn't see her, she still wanted to take the chance to be with him. She didn't know when she would be able to do so again.

They sat there for a while, her watching him and him watching the television. She wasn't sure how much time had passed before her father yawned, stood, stretched his back, and took a step toward the hallway.

A tiny voice entered her head as she watched his movements, a familiar voice that made her skin crawl. She couldn't see Bella, but she heard her warning, crystal clear: "It's not over."

Only a moment passed before her father, still making his way through the doorway, collapsed onto the floor.

Shooting up from her seat, Hazel darted toward him, dropping to the floor beside him.

"Mom! Hurry! Something's wrong!" she screamed to her mother as she cried, her voice meeting no ears but her own. Holding onto his chest, Roman grunted in pain, trying to lift himself, only to fall back onto the carpet.

Desperate, hoping her mother's abilities were honed enough to see her, Hazel headed in the direction of the kitchen. She'd only taken a few steps before a figure in the hallway blocked her path, the darkness enveloping her until the vision faded into oblivion.

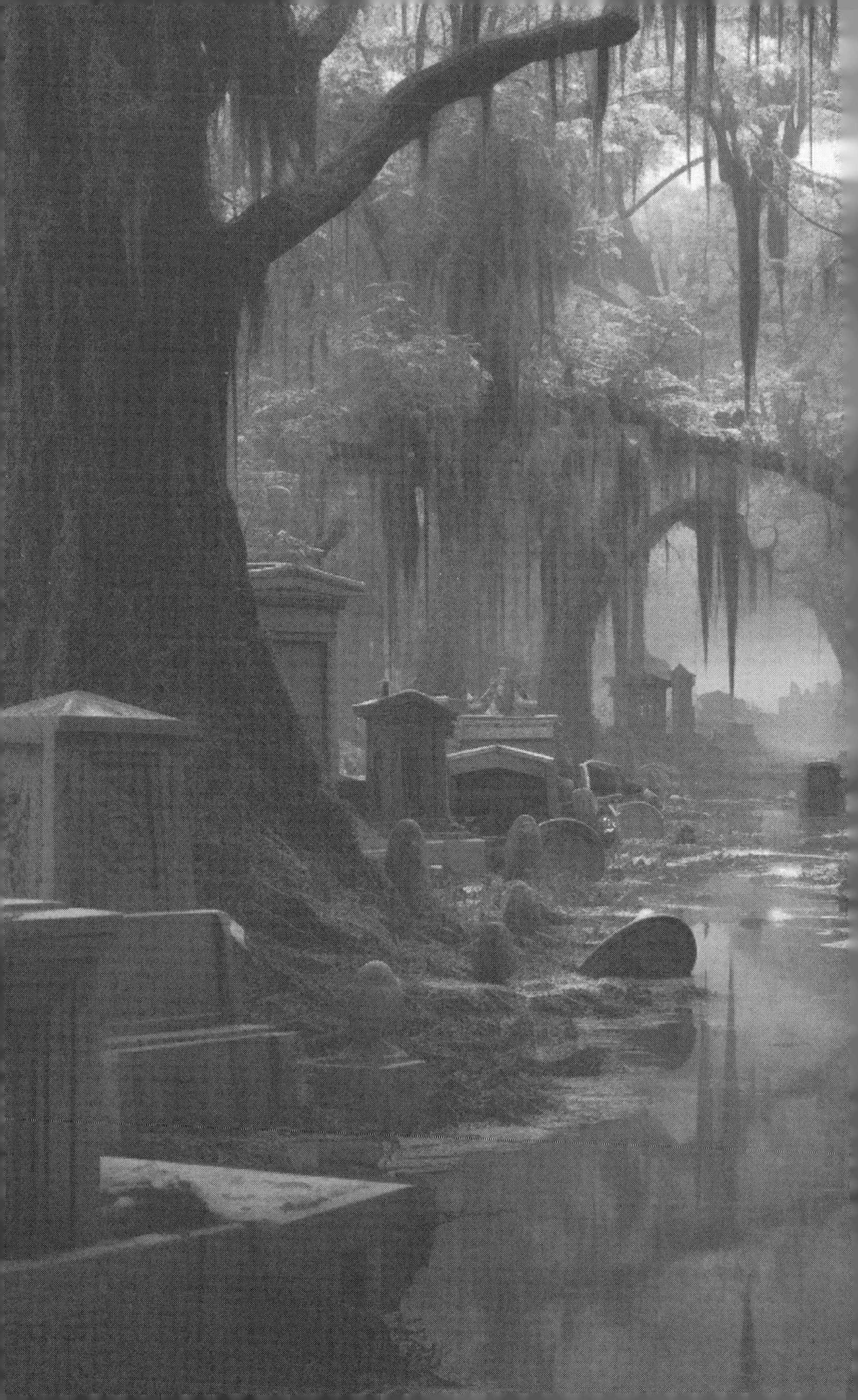

Chapter One
Collector of Souls

Waking up in a cold sweat, Hazel reached for her phone, dialing her mother's number before even checking the time. The spirit-induced dreams plaguing her had grown increasingly ominous, telling her so much yet always leaving her confused. The phone rang several times before the call connected, but there was no greeting, as though whoever answered didn't realize they'd done so.

"Mom? Mom, are you there?"

Muffled voices met her ears a moment before her mother's voice broke through the chaos. "Hazel?" The distress in Sandi's voice opened a pit in Hazel's stomach, one she was well familiar with. Something was wrong. "I'll have to call you back in a little while. Your father collapsed in the den so the EMTs are getting him into the ambulance right now."

For several loud heartbeats, Hazel didn't know what to say. Thoughts and actions warred in her mind, some telling her to catch a plane and fly back to New Mexico, and others telling her she just got back and that she shouldn't jump and do anything. Before she had a chance to get her thoughts straight, sounds of the ambulance pulled her out of her spiral. "Hazel, please don't do anything yet. I'm following them to the hospital and he's stable right now. Once I find out more, I promise to call you and give you an update. Then you can decide what you want to do."

Beside her in the bed, Tate rolled over, rubbing the sleep from his eyes. It was the middle of the night, so she knew her mother was right but waiting for something to happen only ever gave her more anxiety. Still, she knew she wasn't ready to get on a plane–at least not yet.

"Okay, but *please* call me the minute you know more. I need to talk to you about what I saw in my dream. I saw it Mom, and it's not over. I think it's collecting spirits at that crash site." The thought of this entity harvesting souls made her stomach turn but she realized it was possible, even if she didn't understand how.

There were more muffled voices as her mother spoke to the ambulance driver, and then Sandi returned to the phone. "Collecting souls? Are you sure? What did you see? Your father's collapse?"

Running her hand over her hair, Hazel shook her head, her heart beating in deep, echoing pounds that seemed to move her entire chest. "I saw his collapse and I saw Bella and the entity again. It was there, Mom. It was in the house. Almost like it caused something to happen to him or it was waiting to take his soul."

Sandi went silent for a moment, the sound of her getting into her car and turning it on meeting Hazel's ears. "Taking souls like a grim reaper?"

"I really don't think it's a reaper, Mom. I don't know why... It just seems like something else. It seems more malevolent than that, but I can never get the information I need before I wake up."

The cryptic nature of Hazel's dreams caused immense stress to weigh down on her. It was traumatizing for her to watch horrific events happen before her eyes and be unable to stop them. She hated it, but she had yet to find a way to stop seeing them, to stop the spirits from being able to force thoughts and images into her mind.

"Alright, alright." Even though she was clearly trying to maintain her usual calm demeanor, Hazel knew the idea of this dark being in her home was scaring her mother and for good reason. "Try to find out what you can about this entity and I'll update you on your dad. I'll also go through your grandmother's old books and notes when I get back home to see if there's a way to ward our homes to keep this thing out. If it's waiting for souls, I don't want it anywhere near my family."

When the phone call ended, Hazel was left reeling. If anything, she knew she needed to speak to Bella, the seven-year-old child whose mother had been murdered and who clearly had supernatural powers. Speaking with Bella, however, was nearly impossible, at least in real life. The little girl often invaded her dreams, speaking in cryptic messages that Hazel never understood, but there was no way Hazel could contact the little girl's father and tell him what was happening. All that would do was cause Joshua Landry to report Hazel to the authorities for being a crazy person. She'd only just recently told the police about her abilities–well, one in particular, Detective Bourgeois. She wasn't ready to go public and become a pariah.

Sliding his arms around her, Tate urged her to lay back down. She let him. "Is everything okay? Did something happen to your dad?"

The warm strength of his body enveloped her, settling her nerves. "He collapsed tonight but my mom doesn't know what happened yet. The ambulance was taking him to the hospital. I saw it in my dream."

Just thinking about the spirit-induced dream sent a shiver through her body, making her queasy. Tate pulled her tighter, rubbing his hand up and down her back. "Do you feel like you need to go back?"

She shrugged. "After just making that long drive, I don't think I have it in me to make it again, and I'm not ready to fly. Not yet."

"Then there's nothing else to do right now. We can make sure your phone isn't on the do-not-disturb setting and then you should try to go back to sleep. Your mom will call you when they know more."

For a while, Hazel curled into her husband's warmth, staring at the darkness outside the bedroom window. But as the sun peeked above the horizon, she'd fallen into a restless sleep, only to be woken a few hours later by a ringing phone. Before she had a chance to process what was happening, still groggy from sleep, Tate had already picked the phone up.

"Oh, hey, Mrs. Sandi. How is— Okay— Yeah, she's right here."

Pulling herself up on her elbows, she reached out, taking the phone from her husband. With a quick kiss on the cheek, he left the bedroom to give her privacy. She sat up on the bed, placing the phone on her ear.

"Hello."

"It's Mom. Did I wake you?"

The answer to her mother's question was technically yes, but she didn't want her mother to feel like a bother, so she had no intention of answering the question truthfully.

"No. I had to wake up anyway. How's Dad?"

For a few moments, Hazel's mother went quiet as the sound of machines beeping and someone talking in the background met her ears. "He's stable at the moment but being kept under. They think he had another heart attack."

Hearing the words sent Hazel's heart plummeting into her stomach. She'd only just barely rekindled some sense of a relationship with her father. They'd been estranged for years. She wasn't ready to lose him again already, not that she ever could be. "What are his chances? Do they think he'll get better again?"

Without saying a word, Tate entered the room with a steaming cup of coffee in his hand and gave it to Hazel. He really was the best husband in the world and she wondered every day if she was good enough for him. That small gesture of thoughtfulness brought a smile to her face even though her chest was in turmoil. Waiting for her mother to answer the question, Hazel took a sip of her coffee, savoring the rich flavor as it slid down her throat.

"Sorry about that, love," her mother said, breaking the silence. "The doctor popped into the room to speak to me." Sandi hesitated, her voice tinged with exhaustion and worry. "They can't answer your question just yet, sweetie. We will have to first see if he makes it through the day."

When the phone went silent, Hazel still didn't know what she was supposed to do. Living far away from her family had never been a problem; it had actually been more of a blessing. But having her father's life be in jeopardy, especially after they'd reconnected, made it so much more difficult.

She dwelled on her options as she took a shower, needing the water to help wake her up. Of course, her entire thought process was disrupted when a head of luscious red hair popped through the shower curtain. When they moved into Tate's suburban three bedroom home, Hazel thought she would have more privacy from her nosy spectral best friend, especially since Candy had a boyfriend to keep her company, but she always found a way to disturb Hazel at the most inopportune times.

"Didn't you shower last night, doll? How dirty did y'all get?"

Instead of responding, Hazel grumbled and splashed water at her friend, knowing it would go right through her. Candy backed out of the shower, but remained just on the other side.

"I'm just messing with you, love. I heard you talking to your mom. Well, I didn't hear Sandi but I heard your side. How's your dad?"

Turning off the water, Hazel squeezed the excess water out of her hair and opened the shower curtain to grab a towel. She used to be modest when nude in front of Candy, who was a complete bombshell, but she'd eventually gotten over it. "They don't know yet. My mom didn't give me a lot of details yet but she said she would call me once the doctors knew more."

When Hazel left the bathroom, her hair still damp from the shower, Candy and Tate were both in the kitchen, although Tate may have thought he was alone since he couldn't see spirits like she could.

The moment she set her coffee mug on the table, he used the pot to refill it. The way he always took care of her warmed her heart. He truly was the best husband in the world, but she'd stopped saying she wasn't good enough for him since they'd walked down the aisle. If he'd doubted her, he would have never taken it that far.

"I should be home by seven tonight but you'll need to go to the Social Security office and deal with your name change today."

Although she knew he was right, she still groaned. They'd been married for a few weeks already, so she couldn't put it off any longer.

Even as Hazel dreaded driving into the city, a bright smile spread across Candy's cheeks. Hazel turned to her, knowing it was her cue to act involved. "What, Candy?"

Candy only smiled brighter. It was rare that Hazel's moods ever affected her overly excitable friend. "If we have to go downtown…"

"No."

"But you didn't even hear wha—"

"No."

While Candy's face looked as though her puppy had gotten run over by a car, Tate sat down across from her. He was used to their antics. "What does Candy want you to do this time?"

Hazel shrugged, ignoring her friend's pouting. "I don't know but I'm sure it'll be a no. I'm not in the mood to get into any trouble today, at least not while I'm waiting to hear back from my mom."

"I just thought if we were already going to be downtown that we could go say hi to some of our old friends at the courthouse. We haven't been there in a long time."

As she usually did, Hazel repeated Candy's words to Tate since he couldn't hear them.

"Well, if you're around my area at noon maybe we can go to lunch together. I'm sure Bourgeois would like to offer his congratulations in person."

The moment Tate made the offer, Candy's frown turned to a smile. Taking another sip of her coffee, Hazel narrowed her eyes at Candy. "We can go on one condition. You and Jake have to scram when Tate and I are on our lunch date."

Candy nodded, her expression that of a perfect angel. "And I have a condition for you, doll. No bringing home any more spirits. I mean it this time."

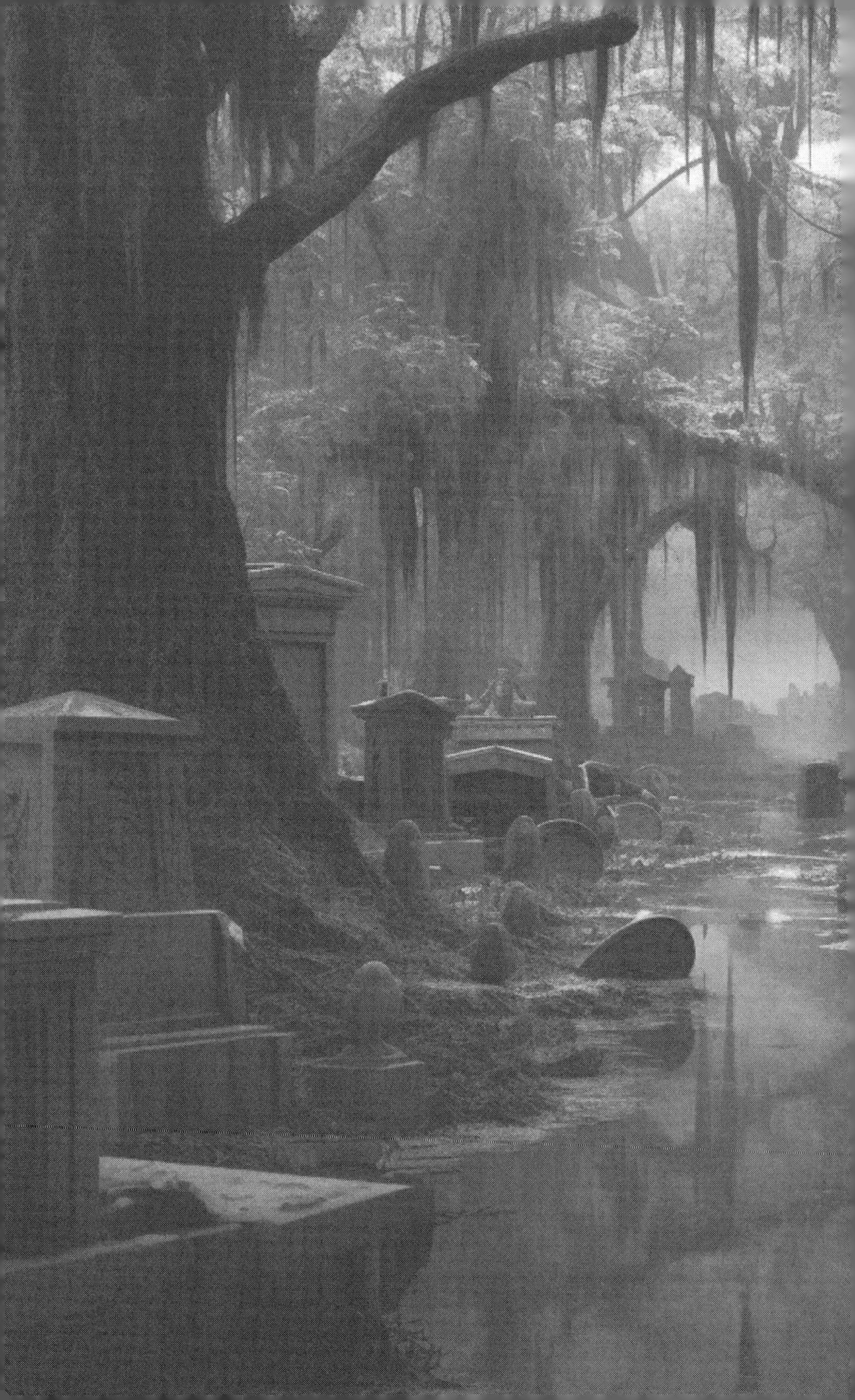

Chapter Two
The Missing Spirits & The Missing Girl

A bowl of cereal and a pep talk later and then Hazel was on her way into the New Orleans traffic with two ghosts in tow. Tate had already left, beating her by about twenty minutes, but they intended to meet up for lunch at the precinct later that day.

Ever since she'd quit her job at the public defender's office, she had stayed far away from that world, so returning to any of the downtown government buildings filled her chest with a burning sense of dread. She knew she would eventually have to return to the city, but remaining in the suburbs had been a welcomed reprieve.

"And no acting up while I'm getting my business done at the Social Security office." After years of being best friends with the feisty spirit, she knew exactly what to expect from Candy when taking her out in public, which was why she often refused to take her. Looking into the rearview mirror, Hazel could see Candy and Jake floating just over the backseat as though they were seated with corporeal bodies.

Candy drew an invisible halo over her head before making the sign of the cross over her chest. "Cross my heart and hope to—oh."

Although Candy thought her joke was funny, no one else in the car laughed, not even her spirit boyfriend. She made a lot of jokes about being dead, but it was a painful reality for all of them, not a laughing matter.

As was always the case, driving into the city took three times as long as it should have, and parking in the downtown area was as challenging as Hazel had remembered. It was why she'd always ended up with parking tickets when she had been an attorney, parking tickets that she would often ask her now husband to get fixed for her.

Finding a place to park several blocks away from the Social Security building, Hazel grabbed all her important documents, checking to make sure her car was parked correctly, before abandoning it and heading toward her first destination.

The fall air was breezy as Hazel walked down Poydras Street, stopping to allow the trolley to pass when she approached the tracks. She smiled at the passengers as they passed, realizing she'd lived in New Orleans for years and had never ridden the historic mode of transportation in the downtown area.

"Are you noticing what I'm noticing, doll?"

Candy's voice caught Hazel's attention when she turned to walk down Magazine Street. "Am I noticing what?"

"I haven't seen one spook since we got out of the car. That's not right. Where are the regulars?"

Halting her steps, Hazel turned to look behind them. "I wasn't even paying attention. Are you sure? You didn't see Ezekial on the corner with his trombone?"

Candy and Jake both shook their heads, Candy's blue eyes wide. "I haven't seen anyone. Something doesn't feel right today. It almost feels...empty."

Icy fingers crawled up Hazel's spine as she scanned the empty street, not empty of people, but empty of ghosts. New Orleans was one of the most haunted cities in the world. It was one of the reasons she'd moved there–so she could help them. Some of the spirits she'd seen every day had been there for hundreds of years.

As Hazel thought back to her dream, and to the conversation she'd had with her mother, Candy and Jake's apparitions flickered, sending her heart into her stomach. "Candy, did you feel the same thing at home? The same emptiness?"

With no hesitation, Candy shook her head. "Not like this. There's something noticeably wrong going on here."

Hazel blew out a breath, thoughts tumbling in her mind. "For now, until I figure out what's going on, I want the two of you to go back home and stay there. I'm going to do what I have to do here, and then I'll be back home soon. I need to talk to some people about this."

Leaving the Social Security office without a moment to spare, Hazel headed to her car so she could meet Tate at the police department. The line to get her legal last name changed to Cormier took the better part of three hours, giving her plenty of time to research on her cell phone, not that she would be able to find anything reliable there. Even if she didn't believe in them, she'd thought about the usual suspects, like the Grim Reaper, who may have come to the city and taken all of the souls away, but why now? She'd been helping spirits cross over her entire life, had seen them her entire life, and had never seen an entire city of spirits just disappear. She had only walked a few city blocks so far, so she knew she may have been worrying for nothing, but it was definitely something she needed to investigate further.

The police station wasn't far from where she'd originally parked, but Hazel still moved her car closer. With storm clouds already darkening the sky, the last thing she wanted to do was run the length of several city blocks through a downpour. In New Orleans, rain was almost always on the menu.

Blowing out a breath, she opened the door to the police station, hoping Tate was ready to go to lunch and not tied up with a case. With the way her day had already been going, she wasn't surprised to find the department in complete and utter disarray.

Ever since the case when she was guided by seven-year-old Bella and her deceased mother, Emily, Hazel had been hesitant to return to Tate's place of employment. That was the case when Hazel had decided to get involved, officially, in the police investigation to help them find the third victim before the killer had a chance to end her life and dump her body in the swamp, just like he had done to the first of two victims. She had never been comfortable sharing her secret; even Tate went nearly ten years of their friendship without knowing she could communicate with the dead. But with so many lives on the line, she saw no other choice but to offer assistance. That case had only been months ago, so it was still fresh in her mind, and it made her hesitant to get involved in another such case anytime soon. Cases with murder victims, especially victims of rapists and serial killers, took a huge toll on her life. With her father sick and the missing spirits, she knew she couldn't juggle anything else.

Still an extreme introvert, even just walking into the station with officers, detectives, and other staff moving up and down the hall, a flurry of conversation going on around her, had her heart beating like a jazz band in her chest. With all the noise, it took a moment before she heard her husband's name. A beat later, there was a light tap on her elbow.

Turning to the side, a middle-age woman with rich brown skin and a head of tight black curls tapped her on the elbow again.

"Are you Officer Cormier's wife?" the woman asked again, this time Hazel catching the entire question and nodding.

Having only been to the station a few times to meet with Detective Bourgeois about Emily's case, she didn't know the woman's name, but her patch had the surname of Boyd, which was a common last name in the community.

"Yes. Is he here? We're supposed to go to lunch together."

Miss Boyd's eyes grew wide as she stood to her full height, which couldn't have been taller than five feet and no more inches, and scanned the room, Hazel following her line of sight.

Not seeing her tall and incredibly handsome husband, Hazel watched as Miss Boyd lifted her two-way radio, asking for his location.

A second later there was static on the device, and from where she stood, Hazel heard Detective Bourgeois' voice when he responded. "If that's his lovely wife, Hazel, please send her to my office. We need her help. She knows Bella, the missing child."

Bella was missing. The words repeated through Hazel's mind like a broken record as she followed Miss Boyd to the detective's office. She knew the way, but with all the commotion, she appreciated the escort. Her hands twisted in front of her as she approached the open door, relieved to only see Tate and the detective waiting for her.

"Hazel." Standing up from behind his desk, Detective Bourgeois lifted his hand toward the empty chair next to her husband. Tate smiled up at her as she sat, reaching over to hold her hand. "It's so good to see you. I wish it was on better terms. Bella went missing last night."

With a half smile, she nodded, her eyes narrowing in on the open file on his desk. She couldn't read the documents, but a picture of the little girl she'd seen in her dreams dozens of times lay right on top of the pile of papers.

Seeming to notice where her attention was, the detective slid the photograph closer so Hazel could pick it up.

Every time Bella visited her in the darkness, the little girl always wore a different outfit, and always had her hair fixed in cute little ways. It was the one thing Hazel always noticed. In the picture, she wore what appeared to be her school uniform, a white shirt with a lace collar, and her dark hair in pigtails.

"Do you remember her?" Detective Bourgeois asked. Tate squeezed her hand gently, letting her know he was there for her, but not interrupting. He knew how hard it was for her to talk about her abilities with others. There was always the fear that they wouldn't believe her, would call her crazy. It had happened many times before, but the police detective had always been open to what she had to say.

As was always the case, she hesitated, not knowing what to disclose. She had a habit of doing her own investigations, and didn't want to disclose anything that could get her into trouble later, but she also didn't want to hold anything back that could delay Bella being found safely.

"Yes. I—um—saw her...but not in person. She comes to me in the darkness. I guess it would make the most sense to say she comes to me in my dreams."

For a moment, the detective went silent, undoubtedly trying to process her unbelievable claims, although he always seemed to believe her. "Kind of how she helped you before...with Hunter's arrest and the plane crash?"

If Hazel were being honest, Bella mostly spoke in riddles, so she often only confused Hazel more. She was a small child with powers she didn't understand, or know how to control, so she wasn't predictable and was rarely helpful.

"I'm not sure how she does it. She seems to not only see what I see, but she's able to interact with me. I didn't start seeing her until her mother's spirit came to me for help. As my powers changed when I came into contact with Emily, I was able to see Bella while she was awake—at least I thought she was awake—and she was able to see me as well. I don't know what it's called, or how she does it, but she does." She blew out a breath, setting the picture back on the desk. "It's always unsettling. When she speaks to me in the darkness, it's almost as though she has more she wants to say, but she can't."

When Hazel looked up, the detective was watching her, twisting the cap on his pen. "When was the last time Bella came to you?"

Closing her eyes, Hazel tried to remember her dream. "I didn't see her last night, not her body anyway. I haven't seen her face in several days, but I heard her voice last night. She spoke to me from the darkness."

Tate slid his arm around her waist, pulling her closer as the detective leaned forward in his chair, steepling his fingers on the desk. "What did Bella say to you last night?"

With her eyes still closed, the tiny voice replayed in Hazel's mind as they passed through her lips, the meaning of them chilling her blood just as they'd done before. "*It's not over.* That's all she said."

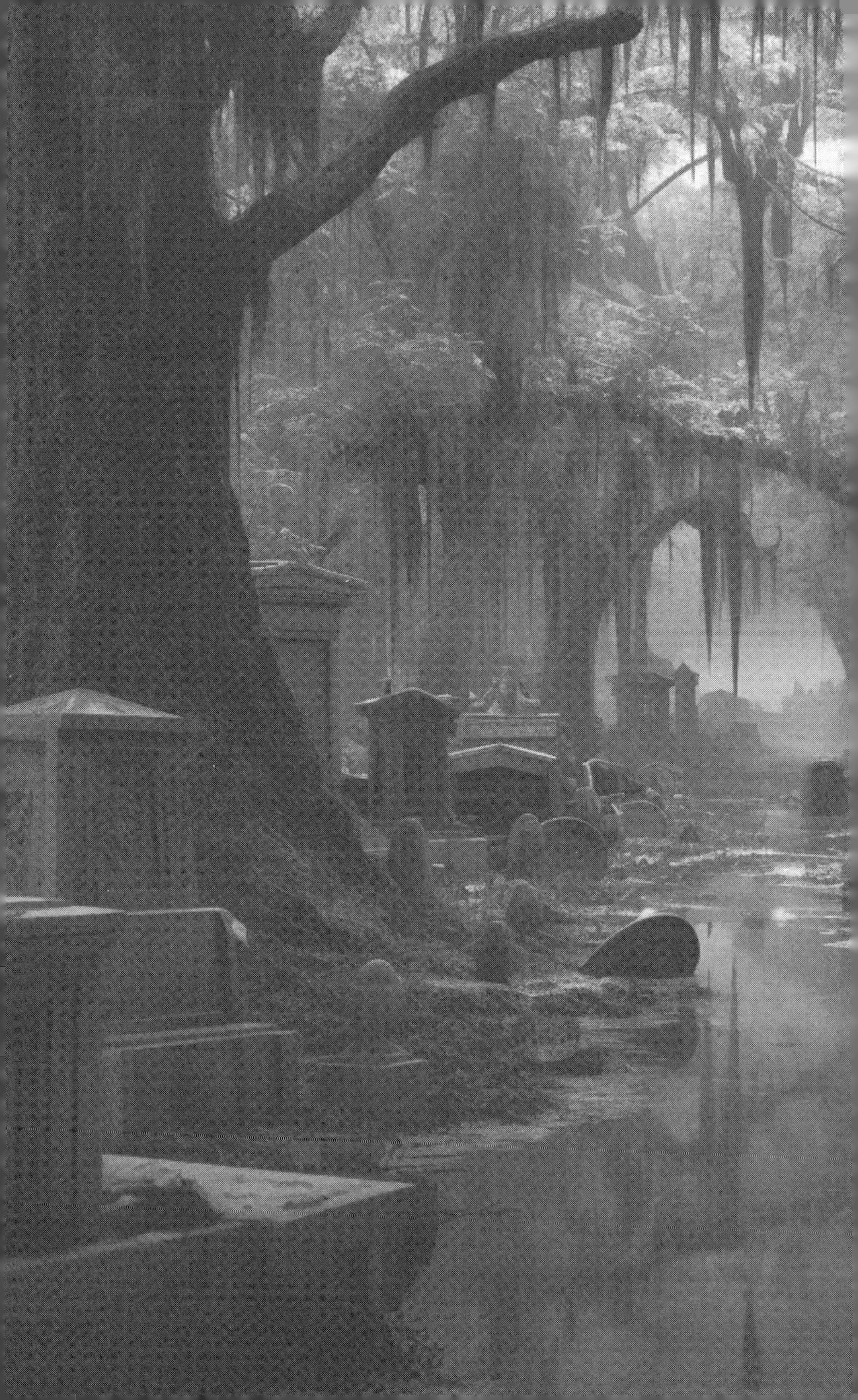

Chapter Three

The Salt Line

The final words Bella had spoken to Hazel hung in the air as they left Hazel's lips, rendering the detective silent for several minutes as he stared at the little girl's picture. Just as Hazel didn't think she could take the silence any longer, he asked "Do you have any idea what she was referring to? *What* isn't over?"

Hazel shrugged, genuinely having no answer. At first, she thought Bella was referring to the dark entity on the plane and on the crossroads, but after finding out Bella was missing, Hazel wasn't so sure. "When she said it, my father had just collapsed. I was watching it happen in my dream somehow, and she'd spoken to me. She could've been talking about my father. She could have been talking about the cause of the plane crash. Or the crimes that took her mother's life." Leaning against Tate, she returned her eyes to the detective. "She could've been warning me about the spirit collector."

After another twenty minutes of explaining the missing spirits to Detective Bourgeois, Hazel was forced to leave the police station without her lunch date. With a little girl missing, Tate was needed to help look for her. Hazel intended to look for Bella as well, but the only way she knew how to was in her dreams.

Leaving the police department, Hazel headed back out of the city knowing the longer she stayed, the worse the traffic would become. On her way home, she stopped at the grocery store to buy salt–a lot of it.

Having the ability to communicate with the dead since she was born, she had never taken stock in the old wives' tales about what repelled spirits and other supernatural entities. As far as she was concerned, all of it was more or less nonsense. But until she knew more about what was causing the spirits to disappear, she wasn't taking any chances with her best friend. So, if a salt line was said to be impenetrable by spirits, she hoped that pouring one around her home would keep Candy and Jake safely inside. Knowing Candy, however, she fully expected her friend to laugh at her for even trying.

When she arrived back home with several bags of salt and explained her theory to Candy, that was exactly the response she'd gotten.

"Are you going to make a line around the house? Like outside? Doll, it rains every day. It'll just wash it away," Candy said as she floated just behind Hazel's back, being anything but helpful. Hazel already knew pouring the salt outside wouldn't work, but she still wanted to pour a line across the entrance to the garage.

"I'm aware of that, Casper. Try to pass through it. If it doesn't work, then I'm wasting my time, anyway."

Leaning over her shoulder, Candy's expression was contemplative. "You missed a spot."

Hazel leaned back on her heels, her back already aching, and she'd only just started. "Yeah. I've missed a lot of them. Try to pass right there and see if you can. I don't wanna pour it everywhere if it won't even work."

Holding her finger aloft, it almost felt like she was scolding a naughty puppy. Knowing Candy, the comparison wasn't far off.

Nibbling on her full bottom lip, Candy floated a few inches forward. "We should wait until Jake comes back so he can try. He's just resting his energy and whoa—"

Her stalling came to a halt as Hazel poured another line of salt around her friend, boxing her in. "I'm guessing you're stuck inside, so it must work?"

Face falling into a scowl, Candy stomped her high-heeled foot several inches above the ground. "Let me out."

Hazel rose back to her knees, shaking her head. "Nope. I think I have stuff to do actually..."

"Hazel, if you don't let me out of here..."

Standing, Hazel moved toward the door, looking over her shoulder. "Just check to see if I missed a spot."

As soon as Hazel walked away from the garage door, her phone rang. Seeing her mother's phone number on the screen sent her heart into its familiar place in her stomach.

Lifting the phone to her ear, fear of bad news numbed her limbs. "Mom?"

Sandi sniffled, sounds of hospital equipment meeting Hazel's ears before her mother's voice did. "Hey, sweetheart." Although Sandi's voice was low and muffled, it sounded like it was more from exhaustion than from grief. "Your dad had another heart attack, but he's stable right now."

"Okay." Lowering herself into a chair, Hazel blew out a breath as some of the feeling came back to her limbs. "Should I fly back right now?"

Just the thought of leaving the missing child and spirits behind to return to New Mexico increased Hazel's heart rate. She was being pulled in two places at once and she didn't know what to do.

"No need to return just yet, sweetheart. There's nothing that can be done other than sit and wait. But if you would like to, I can let you talk to him when they wake him back up."

The television flickered on although the remote control was across the room, telling Hazel that Candy had found her way out of the salt circle.

Ignoring the stunning redheaded specter that stood in front of her with her arms across her chest and a death glare on her face, Hazel stood and turned the television back off. She was more than familiar with Candy's antics. Instead of addressing the ghost in the room, she returned her attention to her mom, who was still waiting for a response.

"I would like that. And when you have time, Mom, there's something I need to talk to you about. It involves what we discussed this morning, but I found out more. Bella is missing."

The call went silent for a moment before her mother responded. "The little girl we saved months ago after her mother was killed—the one you've been seeing in your dreams—she's missing?"

Sandi's voice was no longer low and sleepy, the news clearly affecting her. When Bella had been abducted by her mother's killer, Hazel and her mother had joined forces to help with the case.

"Yes, but that's not the only strange thing that's going on right now. Just as we worried that something was taking the spirits from the plane crash, it appears that something is taking them here as well. Many of the regulars in downtown New Orleans were not there today. I know I need to return to the city and look in more locations, but even Candy said something feels wrong there—ominous. As though something is stealing them to use them."

"Okay… That sounds bad. I hope it's not a reaper, but I'll need to do some research." Sandi went silent again, but Hazel could hear her pacing footsteps through the phone. "For now, keep Candy and Jake away from the city, and try to cross over any spirits you come across. If they're being collected to be used, then they would be better off crossing over. Work with the police—do whatever you can to find that child. Go into the darkness—get hypnotized if you have to—just find her and speak to her. I'll see what I can find out on my end and I'll get back to you really soon."

Hazel made a mental note of her mother's instructions, nodding to herself. "I'll do my best, but this isn't something you need to focus on right now, Mom. You have enough going on with Dad."

As Sandi yawned, the word yes was muffled but understood. "Oh, and Hazel, stay safe. No traipsing through the swamp this time."

"I was going to let you back out," Hazel said before Candy could open her mouth. "My mom called."

Although they often pretended to be mad at each other, Hazel knew better. Scowl falling into something more subdued, Candy lowered herself next to Hazel, wrapping her arm around her friend's shoulders. Candy's touch may have been icy, but it still always gave Hazel comfort. "I know, doll. Jake let me out no sooner than you walked away."

Huffing a laugh, Hazel scanned the living room for the other member of their household, but didn't see him. "That's not surprising. Where did he go?"

Candy shrugged as she ran her fingers through Hazel's hair, the touch like nothing more than a tingle. "I swatted him on his fine ass and sent him to our bedroom like the naughty boy he is. What did your mom say? How is Roman?"

Pulling her feet up on the chair, Hazel wrapped her arms around her knees. Knowing her father was back in the hospital while she was across the country filled her with guilt. They had gone years being estranged and they had only just reunited. If she lost him already, she didn't know how she would recover. "He had another heart attack. Mom said he's stable for now but I could tell by her voice that it's not good. She's exhausted and she's worried. I hope my brother's are making sure she gets some rest."

"So you'll wait to decide if you're going back? I know you're not ready to fly, doll. It's too soon."

Although Hazel realized the same thing, as did her mother, she'd still offered. If it was absolutely necessary for her to get on a plane again, she knew she would deal with it. "I know I'm not ready, but I'll do it if my mom needs me... But even she says I'm needed here, especially with Bella and the spirits missing."

Candy's spectral hand left Hazel's hair as she slid down to the ground at Hazel's feet. "I heard you say Bella was missing but I didn't want to interrupt your conversation. Do the police have any suspects? Anything to go by?"

If Hazel were being honest, her mind had been all over the place when she was in the detective's office, so very little of what was said had sunk into her brain. "As of now, all they know is that she was taken from her home. There will be a big search for her this evening. It's being organized right now. Tate and I intend to join."

Candy's shoulders fell. "This is so much like when we searched for her mother only months ago. Jake and I will help too. You know that."

Hazel's already heavy heart ached, memories of that case haunting her. She and Tate had been a part of the last search party, and she'd also gone on a separate search with the detective and Tate by herself. The swamps of Louisiana were an unforgiving place and she couldn't imagine that little girl being in there somewhere. And to think that Bella was no longer alive and visiting her as a spirit...

Rising from the chair, Hazel bolted into their master suite, barely making it to the bathroom, where she dropped to her knees and retched into the toilet. Candy's icy hand touched the back of her neck as she vomited again.

"It's going to be okay, doll. We'll find her... But I need you to answer one question for me, little bird. Are you pregnant?"

Hazel groaned, not knowing the answer, which only made her vomit again.

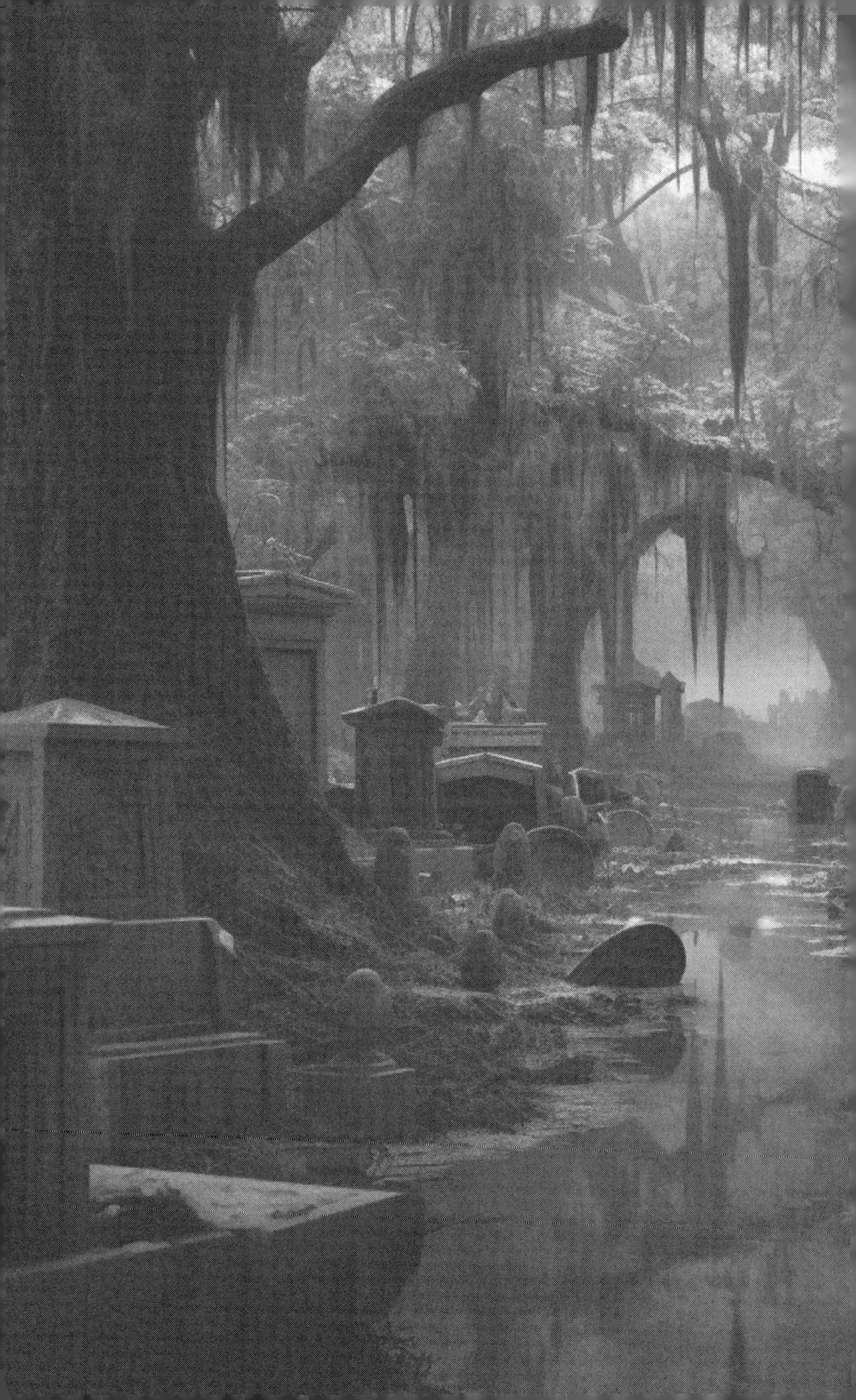

Chapter Four
Gone Without a Trace

Although Hazel wasn't ready to be a mother—wasn't even sure if she ever wanted children—she also realized it was a possibility, especially since she and Tate didn't use protection every time they were intimate. With everything going on, she didn't respond to Candy's question. If she was pregnant, finding out would have to wait until after the search into Bella's disappearance. Between saving a little girl, finding out why there seemed to be an ominous presence in the city and beyond that was collecting spirits, and with her father back in the intensive care unit, she didn't have space for any other stressors on her shoulders. Her posture was terrible enough as it was.

By the time her stomach had been emptied of all its contents, she barely had time to brush her teeth before the garage door opened and Tate walked in. When she turned to look at him from her place at the coffee maker, the curious expression on his face made her nervous about what he would say next.

Setting his gun belt down on the table by the door, he closed the distance between them, pulling her into a hug and placing a gentle kiss on her lips. "My love... Is there any particular reason why salt is all over the garage?"

For the next twenty minutes, Hazel threw together something for them to eat before leaving for the search. She explained what she and her mother had discussed. With Candy and Jake joining them in the kitchen, she also talked to Tate about the missing spirits in more detail than she had with the detective.

Although Candy and Jake offered to help them look for the little girl, just as they had with her mother before, Hazel and Tate finished the salt line around the house before they left, forcing their friends to stay home. Until Hazel knew more about what was going on in the city, she couldn't risk something happening to them. Candy and Jake were part of their family.

With the infamous New Orleans traffic, the trip to Bella's home took much longer than it should have. Tate held

Hazel's hand the entire time, but it didn't ease the tension in her chest. Although they didn't know why Bella was missing, Hazel didn't think the little girl was dead. She had to believe that if Bella was dead, she would have visited Hazel in spirit form immediately. Hazel couldn't think of an explanation for Bella's disappearance, but murder was one possibility she couldn't swallow.

"Do the police think Bella's father has something to do with this?"

Bella's mother, Emily, was murdered by her father's best friend, Hunter. After abducting and murdering multiple women, Hunter kidnapped the little girl and held her as a hostage to avoid arrest. Thankfully, his plan failed, and Bella was rescued before physical harm occurred. Hunter would have been the primary suspect in Bella's disappearance, but he'd been in prison since his arrest, so he couldn't have been involved.

Lowering the radio's volume, Tate took her hand again. "He has been cooperating, but no one has been ruled out as a suspect. According to Josh, Bella disappeared from her bed in the middle of the night. He tucked her into her bed that night and when he went to wake her up in the morning, she was gone."

Hazel felt a sickening chill. Bella had spoken to her in her dream the night before. Knowing Bella was taken out of her warm bed and pulled into the dead of night around that time, she wondered if she'd heard the child's voice before or after she'd disappeared. The thought threatened to make Hazel vomit again.

"Did they find any tracks or footprints—any indication of if she left the house alone?"

If it had been any other child, the thought would have never crossed Hazel's mind, but Bella wasn't like other children. She was wise beyond her years and had superhuman powers that Hazel didn't understand. She didn't know the little girl well, but she knew Bella well enough to know she didn't behave like other seven-year-olds, and Bella was certainly not afraid of the dark.

Arriving at the search area, Hazel was flooded with memories from all the times she'd spent in the swamp over the past few years. The entire property of Bella's home was crowded with people—including the backyard where Bella's mother had spent so much time playing with her before she was abducted and murdered. The last time Hazel had been in that yard, Bella's mother had been there looking over her family and doing her best to help. When Hazel and Tate climbed out of his car this time, however, she didn't see Emily Landry anywhere.

"Her mother's spirit isn't here."

Stepping around to the back of the car, Tate opened the trunk and handed Hazel her rain boots.

"Do you think Emily has been affected by whatever is going on in the city?" he asked.

"I was wondering the same thing."

Hazel scanned the property again as she pulled on her boots, and then placed her tennis shoes back into the trunk. Even with dozens of people on the property, she had no doubt Emily would have found her to help save her daughter. If Emily's spirit wasn't there, something was wrong.

"I need to talk to Bella again, so I can figure out if she is still alive."

She didn't like thinking about such a thing, but it was a possibility whether she liked it or not.

"Maybe she'll come back to you tonight in your dreams."

Closing the trunk, Tate wrapped his arms around Hazel's waist and pulled her close, kissing her on the forehead. "We'll find her, love. One way or another."

She nodded against his chest, savoring the warmth of his body for only a moment before they would venture into the cold swamp.

Turning and walking toward the group of rescuers, it only took a glance for Hazel to notice Detective Bourgeois among the crowd, standing beside Bella's father. While another officer instructed the volunteers, the two men spoke in hushed voices. The detective looked up as Hazel and Tate approached them, dipping his chin in greeting.

The sense of déjà vu filled Hazel with dread. Bella's father's face was twisted into the same emotion. He'd only just lost his wife, and merely months later, his young daughter was missing too. From the look on his anguished face, Hazel couldn't imagine him being involved in any of it, but she knew how evil people could be in secret. He could have been fooling them all.

"Officer Cormier," Detective Bourgeois said, reaching out to shake Tate's hand. "And Hazel. Thank you for coming."

The moment the detective stepped back, Josh Landry stepped forward and reached for Hazel's hand. "I remember the two of you from before…when that psychopath took my Bella. Thank you so much for being here for my family."

When their hands touched, Hazel focused her energy on him, hoping to sense something that would tell her what happened to his daughter, but her abilities didn't work that way.

For months, all she'd wanted to do was call the man in front of her and beg him to allow her to speak with his daughter in person. Meeting with Bella in the darkness rarely gave her any answers, but asking to visit with someone's young child—a child she had no relation to—would have been inappropriate. She wanted to know why Bella continued to visit her dreams, and she wanted to know *how* the seven-year-old was doing it. The problem was, Hazel wasn't even sure if Mr. Landry knew about his daughter's abilities at all. Not even Hazel understood the darkness.

When she let go of Mr. Landry's hand, and turned to listen to the final search instructions, she realized she may have been too late. If they couldn't find Bella—if Bella didn't return to their shared darkness—Hazel would never know what the child with extraordinary abilities was trying to warn her about.

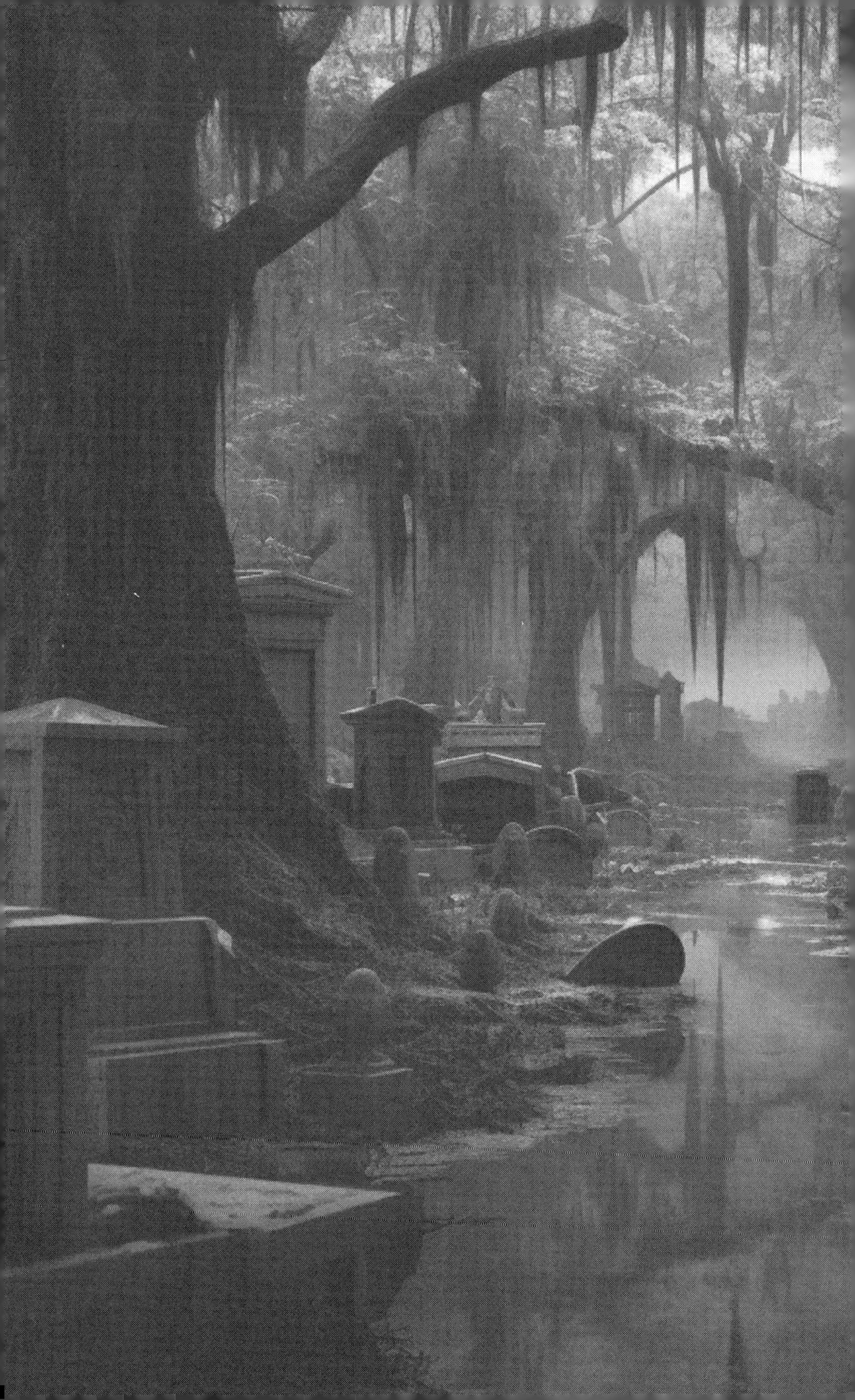

Chapter Five
Return to the Swamp

The first time Hazel traversed the swamp was when she'd been abducted by the serial rapist and killer, Raymond Waters. It was the first time helping a spirit had ever led her into real danger. Since that case, she'd been in one perilous situation after another, and was ready to live a normal life. Well...as normal as it could be with spirits always needing her help.

As she stepped into the swamp with her husband by her side, she felt the mud squish beneath her rubber boots, but she didn't sense any spirits around her. The silence of her sixth sense was unsettling. Although she wanted the spirit demands to settle down, she didn't want the spirits to disappear—not if they were being taken somewhere they didn't want to be.

"Why are they doing this at night?" Hazel turned her flashlight on, shining it ahead of herself and hoping she wouldn't see an alligator. The moss hung like cobwebs from the trees, making the landscape even more eerie.

Interlacing his fingers with hers, Tate pulled Hazel closer and kissed her on the forehead. "Since Bella's disappearance was only discovered early this morning, it took them most of the day to organize something this large, but the police have been out here all day."

She nodded, stepping over a large tree root.

"Remember last time we did this and you brought me to that fancy hotel?" Hazel asked, the thought making her smile. It was the night Tate planned to propose to her, but he'd done it a few days earlier instead because he wanted to give her joy at a time when she was feeling overwhelmed.

From the corner of her eye, she saw his lips lift into a smile. "That was a nice place. We should do that again."

Even though the memory filled her belly with butterflies, the face of the murder victim who'd showed up in the backseat of the car that night momentarily chilled her blood, but the feeling of dread passed before she could barely register it. Huffing a laugh, she stepped closer to Tate until they brushed shoulders, needing his closeness to ease the haunting feeling that washed over her. "We should do it without the ghost in the car next time, though. I may be used to seeing them, but that still scared the shit out of me."

After three hours of searching through the trees and muck, Hazel and Tate headed back to the car. It was simply too dangerous to continue to wander around in the swamp at night. The police and a few of the search groups intended to stay out the entire night, but Hazel was ready to go home. She believed she had a better chance of finding Bella in the darkness of her mind than in the murky water.

When they got back to the car, Tate opened the trunk, helping her change her shoes. Their boots were disgusting, but he was always prepared. As Hazel slipped on her clean shoes, Tate placed their dirty ones into a garbage bag before putting them back into the trunk so he could clean them when they got home.

Climbing into the car, she took one more glance at Bella's home, her heart wrenching at the thought of what could've happened to the little girl. She knew Bella was smart, as well as powerful, but she was still a seven-year-old child, and no small child could be safe all alone in the swamp.

She thought about what could have happened to Bella for much of the ride home, but as they got closer, her thoughts changed, and she began to think about what Candy had asked her that morning. It wasn't something she thought she was ready for—pregnancy—but she knew her husband was. Until she knew for sure, however she didn't want to tell him and get his hopes up. When he went back to work, she intended to go to the store and buy a test.

After driving through very little traffic, they pulled into the driveway just before midnight. Wondering if she was pregnant only made her want to call her mom again, but it was too late. With everything Sandi was dealing with, Hazel didn't want to wake her if she'd finally gone to sleep, so she resigned herself to talking to her mom in the morning.

Although Hazel was too exhausted to shower, the swamp smell that had infiltrated her hair and skin made it absolutely necessary. So, when they arrived home, she went straight to their master suite, Tate following at her heels.

"I'll start the water," he said, walking around her as she dug in her dresser for clean pajamas. Unlike her best friend, who undoubtedly had an obscene amount of sexy lingerie in her invisible, ghostly wardrobe, Hazel's pajamas mostly consist of T-shirts and boxer shorts. They were comfortable, and her husband didn't seem to mind. He hadn't married her for her fashion sense.

By the time she got into the bathroom, Tate was already naked and standing in front of his sink as he brushed his teeth. Her blood heated as she took in his muscular form, her body telling her that sleep would have to wait.

Soft sobs echoed through the darkness, pulling Hazel further into the abyss, when all she wanted to do was turn around and run.

"*Bella?*"

The place she called the darkness—where the little girl had been finding her for months in her dreams—was not always dark. It wasn't even a place. Although she'd been there several times, Hazel wasn't sure what it was, or if it was even a dream at all. They'd met on the plane many times. This time, however, there was nothing but emptiness.

Wrapping her arms around herself, Hazel tried to rub warmth into them, her entire body affected by her unease. As she stepped forward, her bare feet dragging across the stone floor, she couldn't make out where she was. She couldn't see anything, but the sniffle was unmistakable.

"Bella?"

As though they'd heard her, the crying stopped, Hazel holding her breath as she listened for a response. Moments later, something scraped against the floor somewhere to her right, not quite close enough to determine what it was.

"Hazel?"

Breath catching in her lungs, Hazel froze, widening her eyes to peer into the darkness, but it was useless. It was as though the place had sucked up every ounce of light.

"Bella, where are you? Everyone is looking for you." Tears burned the backs of her eyes as she held her hand out before her, hoping to feel what her eyes couldn't see. "Please, Bella, help me find you."

"Shush." Bella's shushing her was just above a whisper—so low Hazel almost missed it. "We have to be quiet, Hazel. They're always listening."

A chill went down Hazel's spine, her body instantly aware they weren't alone. Fear gripped her, halting her steps as a heartbeat quickened.

"Bella," she whispered. Her eyes continued to scan her surroundings, seeing nothing but opaque blackness.

"Who's listening, Bella? Where are we?"

As she waited for the child to answer, icy fingers grabbed her arms, a dozen hands, pulling her back the way she'd come. She didn't need to see them to see what was forcing her away from the child. After a lifetime of being haunted, she knew the feel of ghostly hands when they touched her.

"Sweetheart. Hazel, wake up."

Although Hazel wanted to wake when Tate's voice called to her, she was too cold—her body too heavy and numb to function.

"Sweetheart, I need to get your fever down or I'll have to take you to the emergency room. Here." Tate's fingers prodded at her lips, pressing two pills between them before holding a glass of water up to her mouth. "Drink some water, sweetheart. I need you to take this medicine."

Her body trembled, her teeth chattering as she tried to swallow the pills down. Slowly, the pressure pulling her body into the bed ebbed, allowing her to open her eyes.

Worry creasing his face, her husband sat next to her on the bed, Candy and Jake floating behind him. She tried to sit up, but she couldn't.

"T-Tate?" The chatter of her teeth made her voice tremble. "Tate, what's wrong?"

Brushing her hair away from her face, Tate leaned over to kiss her on the forehead.

"You're burning up, sweetheart. You were thrashing and talking in your sleep. When I woke up to check on you, you were hot enough to burst into flames."

She reached for the blanket, needing warmth, but he pulled it away.

"Your temperature is 104 right now, love. I need to get you into the bathtub. If we can't break it, I'll have to take you to the hospital."

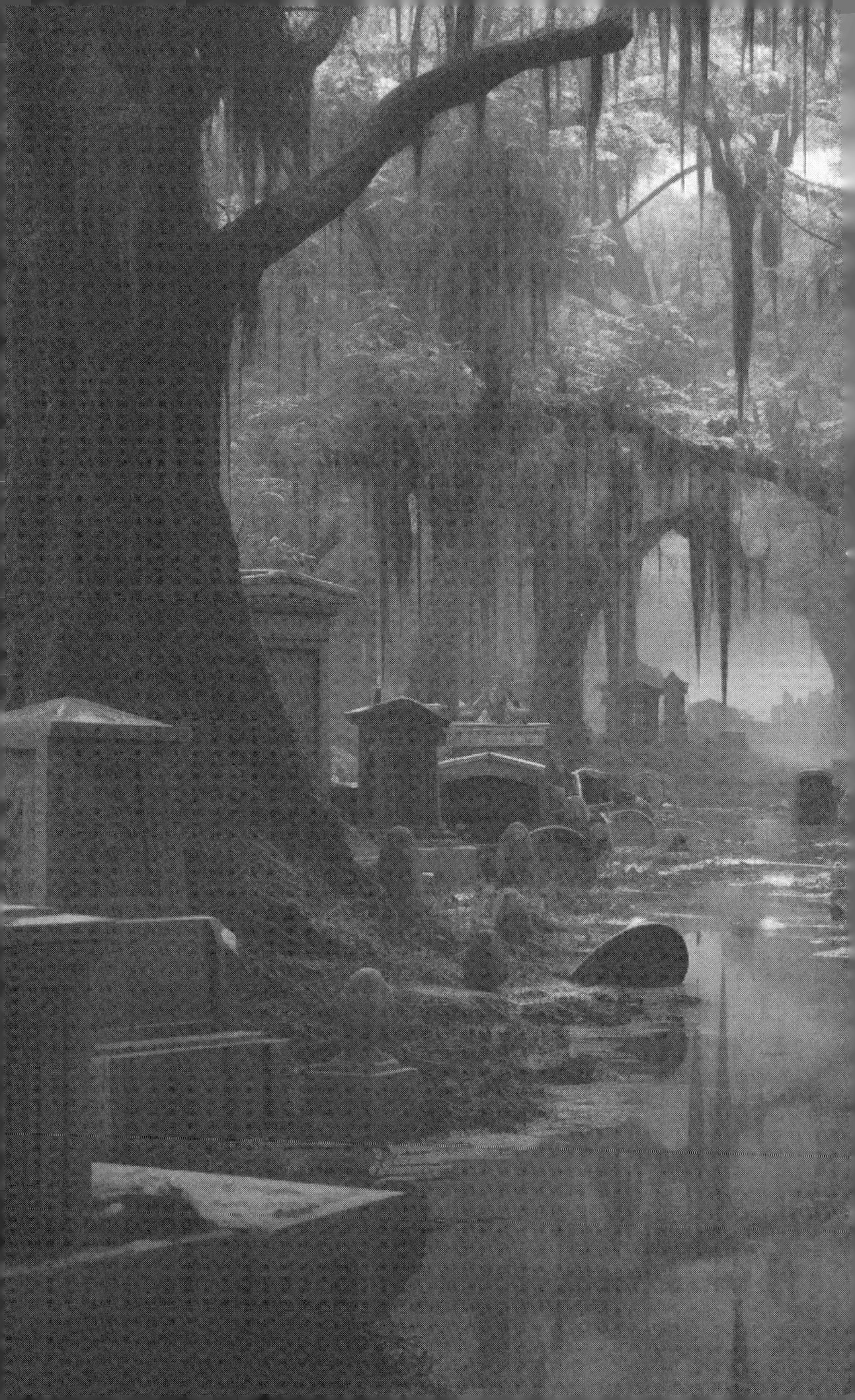

Chapter Six

Congratulations

"I promise you I'm fine." Buckled into the passenger seat of Tate's sedan, Hazel wrapped her arms across her chest like a petulant child. "I don't need to go to the doctor."

Turning a momentary glance to her, Tate grinned, his dimples on full display. "Do you know what you sound like right now? A kid trying to get out of school. Your temperature was through the roof last night, so you're going to the doctor."

Fluttering her eyelashes at him, she smiled from ear to ear. "If I'm a good girl, will you take me for ice cream?"

Tate chuckled, reaching over to hold her hand. "I can absolutely take you for ice cream afterwards, but only if you're a good girl."

Hazel huffed, turning to look out the window at the mid morning traffic. The doctor's office was local, but most of New Orleans' suburbs dealt with traffic during rush hour. "I'm always a good girl."

When Tate barked a laugh, Hazel feigned offense, but she knew the truth. Even as an adult, she always found a way to get herself into trouble.

Pulling up to the doctor's office twenty minutes later, it only took a few moments to be brought back to a room and for the doctor to come in to see her. Hazel had expected the visit to be brief, because she did, in fact, feel fine. After Tate had gotten her fever down in the middle of the night, she'd returned to bed and awoke with no more fever. She thought it would only be a short doctor's visit, but after the doctor checked her ears, nose, and throat, making sure there were no infections from ailments that were common that time of the year, the doctor seemed stumped. When he handed Hazel's file to the nurse, and ordered a full battery of tests, Hazel wasn't sure what he was looking for but her stomach churned anyway.

"I told you I was fine." Knowing she was about to get poked with needles brought Hazel's grumpy mood back full force. "You're going to owe me two scoops after this."

Wrapping her in a hug, Tate pressed his lips to hers, the touch making butterflies take flight in her belly. "You can have as many scoops as you want, love. Let's just make sure everything checks out first."

For the next fifteen minutes, the nurse filled up several tubes with Hazel's blood, nearly sending the contents of her stomach to the floor.

It wasn't until she sat on the toilet with a little plastic cup in her hand that she realized the doctor was checking to see if she was pregnant. A numbing chill washed over her, halting her movements. When she found out the truth, it would become her reality, and she didn't know if she was ready for that.

"Hazel?" Tate called out through the closed door, startling her back into the present. "Are you okay?"

"Y-yeah. I'll be right out."

Trying to pull herself together, she did her business, setting the sample cup in the little window and leaving the bathroom. Tate waited just outside, a questioning look lingering on his face. There wasn't much Hazel could hide from him. He knew her better than she knew herself. "Are you sure you're okay?"

Even though she most certainly was not okay, she nodded and slipped her hand into his.

With all her tests complete, she and Tate returned to the room and waited for the doctor to release her. As they waited, a knot tightened in her stomach, anxiety making it difficult to breathe. The only thing easing the weight on her shoulders was knowing her father was still in stable condition, although there were no guarantees he would stay that way.

Lost within her thoughts as she stared down at her and Tate's interlaced hands, she jolted when the doctor walked back into the room, sitting on his rolling stool.

"All right, Hazel, we have a few results back, but we will have to wait on the blood test results. The nurse will call you with those results later today or tomorrow." He twisted on his stool, smiling up at her. "I can't say I know yet why you ran such a high fever last night, but I do have an explanation for your nausea."

Heart hammering against her rib cage, she knew the reason before the words even left his lips.

"I hope this is happy news for the two of you, but your pregnancy test was positive."

The words hit Hazel's stomach like a lead weight, sending her throwing herself across the room to vomit into the trash can.

Dropping to his knees beside her, Tate pulled her hair away from her face, taking a damp napkin from the doctor and wiping her face.

"I'll get you a prescription for your nausea and prenatal vitamins," the doctor said, standing and moving toward the door. "I'll see if we have anything with ginger also. When you're feeling a little better, I'd like to get an ultrasound."

Hazel fell back on her heels, dry heaving as the doctor stepped out of the room.

"Any better, sweetheart? Can I get something for you?"

Shaking her head, she leaned against Tate's side, melting into him when his arm went around her shoulders.

"Are you happy?"

Although she already knew the answer, Hazel's question was hesitant, because she was more unsure of her own answer, than his.

Tate pulled her closer, kissing her on the temple. "Of course, I am, but what matters more is how you're feeling about it. I know it wasn't planned."

Not wanting to lie to him, she shrugs. "I'm not unhappy—just shocked, I suppose."

As they sat on the floor, Hazel's nausea finally fading, the nurse entered the room, giving her a cup of what smelled like ginger tea.

"That should help with your nausea. Do you need more time, or are you ready for your ultrasound?"

Hazel nodded, allowing her husband to help her off the floor. "As ready as I'll ever be."

Following the nurse to the ultrasound room to see her baby for the first time, all Hazel's other obligations fled her mind. An unexpected pregnancy would undoubtedly throw a wrench in things, but she realized by the genuine smile on Tate's handsome face that it wasn't a bad thing.

The ultrasound room was dimly lit, with a large monitor on one wall. Hazel lay down on the exam table and the nurse squeezed a lubricant on the transvaginal ultrasound device. Just looking at it made her cringe, but she realized she was being silly. A moment later, the doctor walked into the room and the nurse moved over, giving him access to the ultrasound machine.

Staring at the blank ceiling, her mind raced. She couldn't believe that she was going to be a mother. It was all so surreal. She had always been so careful, so meticulous with her birth control. But somehow, she'd gotten pregnant.

Tate stood by her side, holding her hand tightly. As the doctor started slipped the device inside her, the feeling anything but comfortable, a wave of anxiety washed over her. She watched the screen, the images having no recognizable shape, and then there it was—the tiny flicker of a heartbeat.

Hazel gasped, tears welling up in her eyes. She had never felt such a mix of emotions before—fear, wonder, excitement, and love all battling for dominance in her heart.

Tate squeezed her hand even tighter, his own eyes misty with emotion. "That's our baby."

Turning to face them, the doctor smiled. "Congratulations, you two. Everything looks great so far."

When Hazel and Tate left the doctor's office with four small pictures of their unborn baby, who looked like nothing more than a peanut, Hazel's unease started to fade. For the first time in her life, she had something to look forward to—something to protect and love unconditionally. Despite the unexpected nature of her pregnancy, she knew in her heart that she was capable of being a good mother. She was still a bit in shock, since having children was something she and Tate had yet to discuss, but she loved her husband, and his joy at the news was infectious.

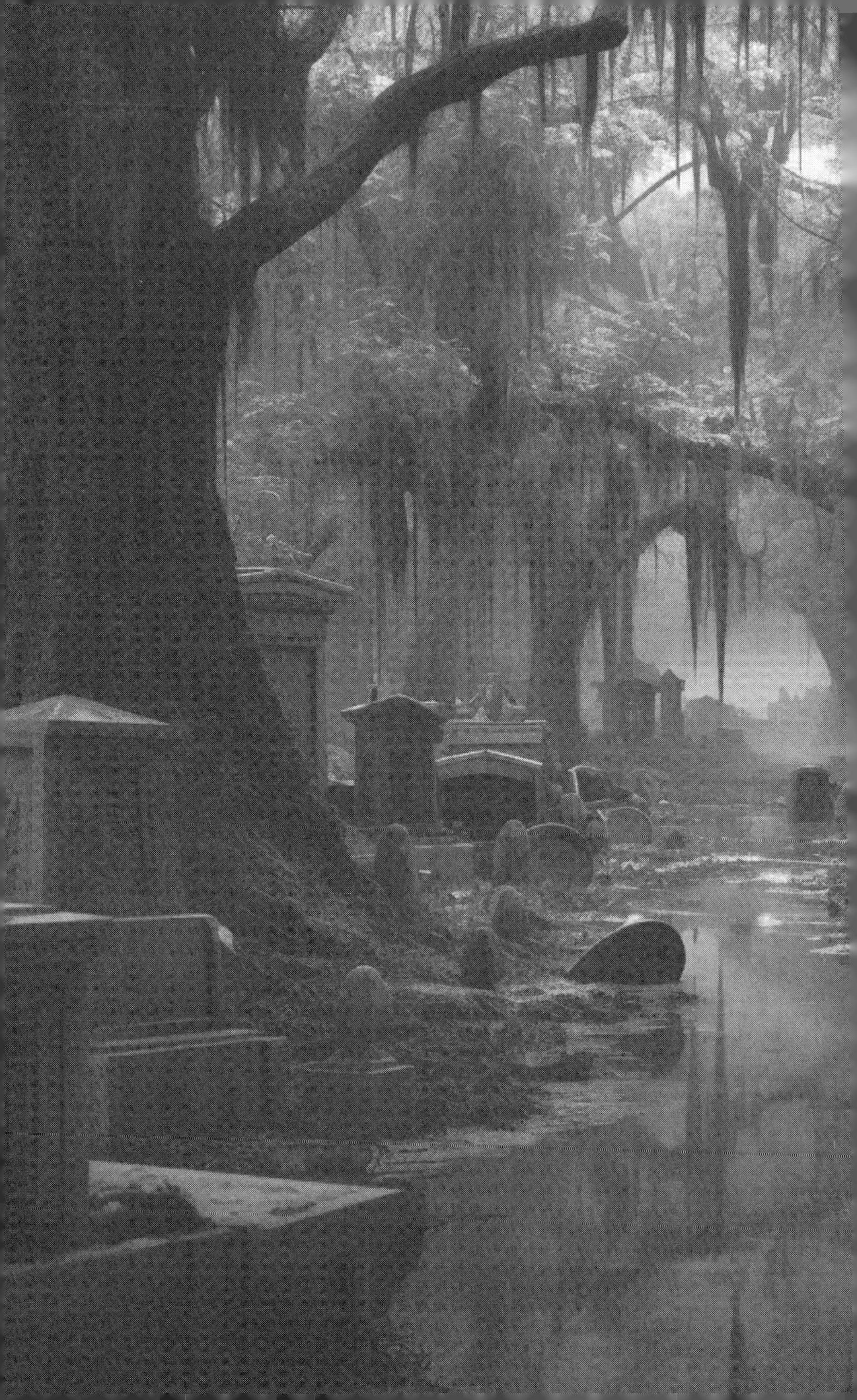

Chapter Seven
Sharing the News

Hazel and Tate arrived home less than an hour after leaving the doctor's office. Although she'd asked for ice cream on the way to the doctor, the truth was that she was too nauseated for sweets. All she wanted on her way home was fries. So, healthy or not, Tate pulled into a drive-thru and bought some for her.

When they arrived home, shock and disbelief still numbed Hazel's limbs. Getting pregnant wasn't something she expected-or even something she knew she wanted. Now she would have to share the news with her mother and best friend, which admittedly made her nervous. However, with her father in intensive care, she didn't want to share the news with her mother yet. There was no doubt her mother would be thrilled, but it was a lot to process all at once, for all of them.

Tate held his hand on the small of her back as she walked in through the garage door, nausea still roiling in her stomach.

The moment they entered the living room, Candy was sitting on the couch in the living room, her feet propped up on the armrest as though she had a corporeal body. Her lover, Jake, was not in the room, but that was not surprising, since he still had less control over his spiritual form than Candy did.

The moment the fiery redheaded spirit noticed them, a sly grin spread across her face.

"So," Candy said, "what's the good news?"

Hazel was too overwhelmed to answer immediately, and instead stared at her friend, her mouth slightly agape.

"Come on," Candy said, raising an eyebrow. "Spill it."

Taking a deep breath, Hazel tried to compose herself. "You were right. I'm pregnant." Without her permission, a smile slowly spread across her face.

Candy's eyes widened in surprise, and then she broke into a wide grin. "Oh my gosh! That's amazing! Congratulations!" Floating off the couch, she surged across the room, wrapping icy arms around Hazel's neck. "I can't believe it!"

Unable to help but feel a bit of excitement herself, Hazel laughed, even though her own emotions were all over the place.

"So," Candy said, a mischievous glint in her eyes, "when are you due?"

Hazel laughed. "The doctor said April."

"Oh! Right before hurricane season!" Candy's grin widened. "When you think about it...it's kind of fitting. This is going to be so much fun! We have so much to plan for. I can't wait to be an auntie!"

Always knowing his cue to leave, Tate kissed Hazel on the temple and walked into their bedroom, closing the door behind him. Candy, with her hands gripping Hazel's forearms, never skipped a beat.

"We're going to have to find some cute baby clothes. Oh. My. Gosh. Are those ultrasound photos?"

Hazel nodded, pulling the pictures out of her bag. "It's still hard to believe." When Hazel lowered herself onto the sofa, Candy leaned in for a closer look.

"I'm so excited for you." Running her pale fingers along the perimeter of the picture, Candy's eyes glistened with spectral tears. "You and Tate will be amazing parents."

Hazel felt her own eyes fill with tears. Despite the initial shock, she was starting to feel excited about the prospect of bringing new life into the world, and it was heartwarming to have her best friend by her side.

"Thanks, Candy." Even with her friend's freezing form beside her, Hazel's insides were warm. "I couldn't do this without you."

In her usual fashion, Candy rolled her eyes, but then flashed a beaming smile, hugging Hazel again. "Of course, you couldn't. That's what best friends are for."

As Hazel pulled away, she couldn't help but feel grateful. Grateful for her husband, for her best friend, and for the little one growing inside of her.

With Hazel and Tate taking a three hour nap, the rest of the afternoon went by quickly, and before they knew it, the sun was already setting outside their windows. Once they climbed out of bed and ordered Chinese delivery, sitting on the sofa to eat while watching one of their favorite competition cooking shows, Hazel was already tired again. She'd sent a few text messages to her mother, but hadn't mentioned the pregnancy. With everything that was going on with her father, she didn't think it was the right time. When her father woke, that was when she intended to share the news with both her parents together. At that moment, he was no better or worse than he had been the day before, so it was just the wrong time.

By the time they were leaving the living room to take a shower, Hazel could tell that something was wrong with Candy. Her friend had been so excited that morning about the baby, but for the past few hours, her mood had shifted.

Allowing Tate to go into the bedroom without her, Hazel stayed behind so she could talk to Candy, who was hovering just over one of the reclining chairs in the living room.

"Hey. Are you okay?"

When Candy's big blue eyes turned up to meet Hazel's, Hazel had no doubt something was bothering her. She lowered herself to the edge of the chair.

"Candy, what's going on?"

Shrugging, Candy slumped down into the chair. "I know Jake's energy is unstable, but I haven't seen him all day, and that's unusual. With everything going on...with the missing spirits...I'm worried something happened to him."

Hazel's heart dropped into her stomach, squeezing uncomfortably at the thought that whatever this thing was that had struck so close to her home. "And the salt...the salt didn't work?"

Lifting one shoulder halfheartedly, Candy wiped a sparkling tear from her cheek. "I thought it was working but maybe he just wasn't strong enough."

Unsure what to say, Hazel leaned back in the chair beside her friend, thinking for a moment. "It's too late right now, but I'll go see Miss Celeste again. I'll try to find out something. We will get him back. I promise."

Hazel stepped onto the porch of the small cottage the next day with a heavy heart. She had come to seek the advice of the elderly Wiccan, Celeste, on a matter of the utmost importance, although she had still yet to visit Celeste just to have tea. Life had simply been too busy for social calls. Still, she knew Celeste would likely have some information that could help her.

When Celeste opened the door, her light eyes bright and long hair left down and flowing, she wore the same type of layered bohemian clothing Hazel always admired. On this day, Celeste wore an ankle length patchwork skirt with a mauve blouse and a brown ankle length cardigan layered on top. The home looked the same as well. The air was filled with the smell of incense, herbs, and spices, and the walls were lined with shelves and cabinets containing various crystals, bottles, and tools. In the far corner was an altar, draped with tapestries and lit with candles. All around her, the air was alive with the hum of energy, buzzing against her skin.

Greeting her with a lined, yet beautiful, grin, Celeste motioned to the chairs in the tea room. "Come in, my dear. Sit down and tell me what has brought you here today."

Taking a seat, Hazel told Celeste about the spirits that were disappearing. "I can't explain it—it seems as though they were just vanishing into thin air. I was hoping you could offer some insight."

Celeste nodded slowly. "It sounds like someone has been practicing an old form of necromancy—summoning spirits to do their bidding, but I admit there could be other explanations." Her bright eyes looked into Hazel's, her expression turning serious. "Whatever the cause, there are ways to protect the spirits from such a fate. We must call upon the power of the elements, the energy in the earth that comprises everything we see, feel, and hear."

Hazel leaned forward, eager to hear more. Celeste's words had given her hope that she could put an end to the strange occurrences that were plaguing the city. She watched as Celeste reached for a small wooden box on the shelf beside her.

"This is a special blend of herbs and oils that will help ward off any dark spirits that may be lurking." Opening the box, Celeste sprinkled some of its contents into a bowl. She then lit a match and set the mixture ablaze, causing a burst of fragrant smoke to fill the air.

Hazel breathed in the scent, feeling a sense of calm wash over her. As the smoke twirled through the air in a dancing tendril, Celeste gestured for Hazel to come closer and placed her hands on Hazel's head. Hazel felt a warmth spread from her scalp to the rest of her body as Celeste began to chant.

After several minutes, Celeste removed her hands, the smoke dispersing in the air. "You are now protected from the evil spirits. But be warned, Hazel. The forces at work are stronger than you may realize. You must be careful in your journey ahead."

Hazel nodded, taking in the gravity of the situation. She knew that she was up against powerful forces, and that she would need all the help she could get.

"I understand," she said, standing up from the couch. "Thank you, Celeste. Your guidance means a lot. But there is something else."

Nodding, Celeste took a sip of her tea, waiting for Hazel to speak. "The young girl who visits my dreams, Bella. She's missing."

Leaning forward in her chair, Celeste reached for Hazel's hand. "Remember what I've taught you before. When you see her again, there will be signs of where she is—of what she wants you to see. Pay attention to everything. There is a strong chance that the missing spirits and the missing girl are related. As I said before, these things are dangerous. So you must be careful."

Hazel licked her dry lips, nausea turning her stomach as she tried to process Celeste's words.

"Remember, Hazel, the spirit world is a delicate balance. It is up to us to protect it."

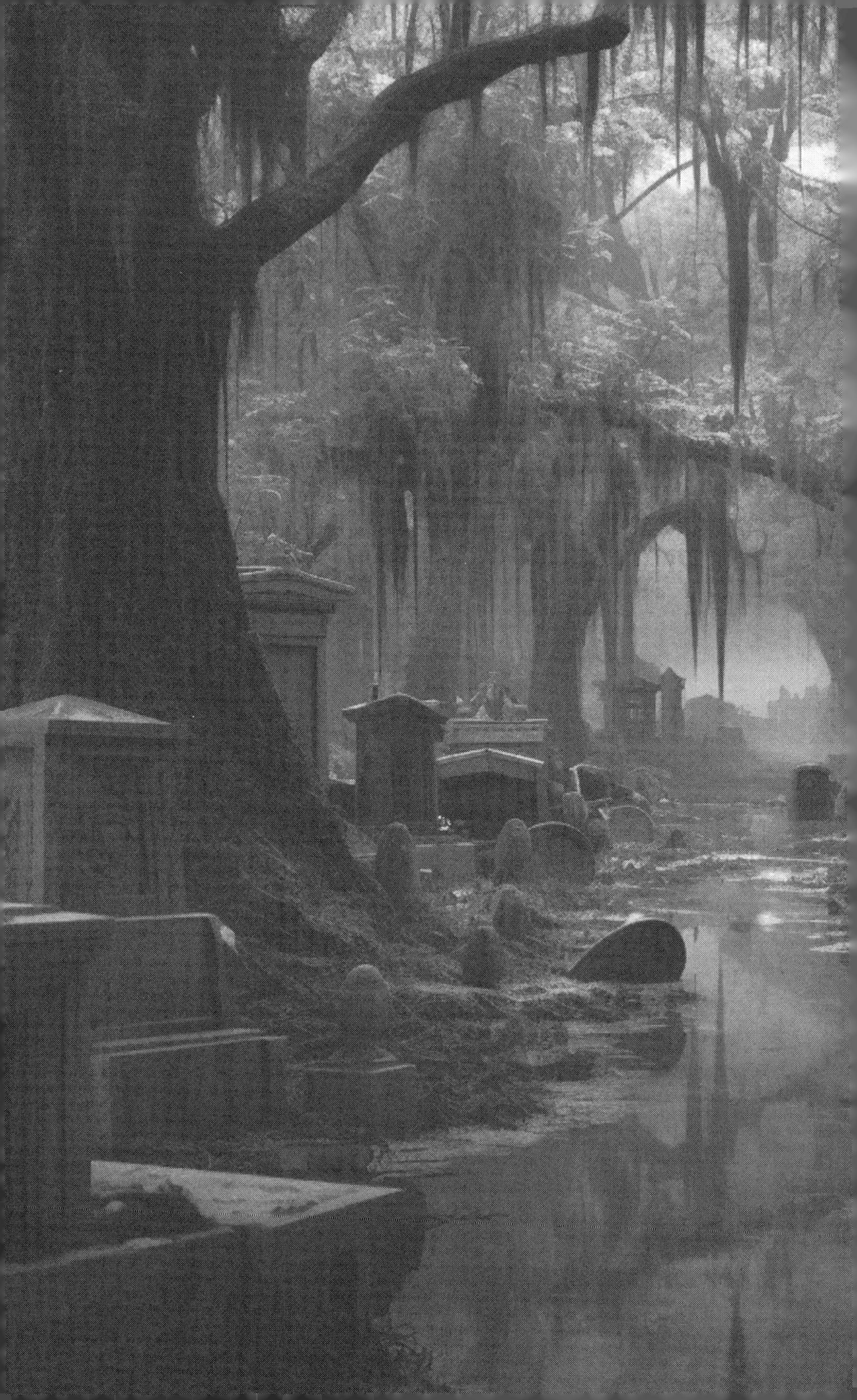

Chapter Eight
The Void

After leaving Celeste's cottage, Hazel returned home, nausea causing her to pull over and vomit on the side of the road. Her morning sickness was only getting worse. With everything she needed to do, all the weight on her shoulders, she didn't have time to be sick. Not that anyone ever did.

To everyone's dismay, Jake did not reappear that evening. Ever since he was murdered, Jake had always had a difficult time regulating his energy, causing him to disappear for brief periods of time. He wasn't as strong of a spirit as Candy was, but this was different. He was gone and Candy was devastated. They all were.

Fearing for Candy's safety, Hazel and Tate decided to redouble their efforts and lay down more salt and herbs from Celeste, hoping the concoction would protect their friend.

With all of that done, and no new leads on Bella's case, Hazel and Tate turned in to bed early, since Tate had to return to work the next morning.

As Hazel lay in her bed, with Tate sleeping soundly at her side, the moonlight cast an ethereal glow through the thin curtains, as though the spirits were trying to find their way in. Closing her eyes to blot out the light, she thought about Bella, hoping to find the little girl within the darkness again.

After a while, the clamor of her day faded away, replaced by the soft whispers of the wind outside her window. Her breathing slowed, and her body relaxed, sinking deeper into the embrace of her unconscious mind.

As she entered the realm of dreams, Hazel found herself surrounded by an otherworldly landscape that seemed to exist on the very edge of reality. Mist swirled around her like tendrils, reaching out to touch her skin before dissipating into nothingness. Shadows loomed at the corners of her vision, their shapes

shifting and changing with every passing second. The air was thick with a palpable energy that Hazel could feel pulsing through her veins, heightening her senses and tying her inexplicably to this place.

This was no ordinary dream. It was a world where the boundaries between the living and the dead blurred, where spirits roamed freely alongside the thoughts and memories of those who slept. Hazel knew that somewhere within the spectral realm she found herself in, Bella would be waiting for her. The urgency of her quest filled her with a fierce determination, fueling her every step as she navigated the ever-changing terrain in search of the little girl.

The mist grew denser as Hazel ventured further into the unknown, its cold fingers brushing against her face like icy breaths from a ghostly presence. Despite the chill, she pressed onward, her heart pounding with the knowledge that Bella needed her. She would not let anything stand in her way, not even the darkness that threatened to swallow her whole.

"Come on, Hazel," Bella whispered softly in the back of her mind, urging her to keep moving. "You're almost there."

"Where are you?" Hazel cried out, her voice cracking with fear and desperation as she stumbled through the murky landscape, the ground beneath her feet almost

like sodden grass, but it was too dark to tell. The weight of her concern for Bella threatened to crush her, but she pushed it aside, focusing on the task at hand.

"Please, show yourself!"

The shadows seemed to pulse around her, as if they were alive and reacting to her pleas. Hazel's breaths came in shallow gasps, each one a struggle as the dense fog filled her lungs. She knew that time was running out, and she couldn't afford to lose herself within the dreamscape.

"Stay focused," she reminded herself, her thoughts racing even as her body grew weary. "Bella needs me."

And then, like the first rays of sunlight breaking through the clouds, a faint glow appeared in the distance. It shimmered and danced, drawing Hazel's attention like a beacon of hope amidst the darkness.

Hazel hesitated, unsure whether to trust her eyes. But in her heart, she knew it could only be one person—Bella.

"Follow me," the glowing figure beckoned, the voice echoing across the dream world, reverberating through the very fabric of reality itself. There was no mistaking that voice. It was the same one that had been her lifeline, her anchor, in the darkness.

"Wait!" Hazel called, forcing her exhausted legs to move faster as she chased after the spectral apparition. The mist seemed to part around her, allowing her passage as she raced towards the light. Her determination burned like a fire within her, driving her onward despite the gnawing fear that clawed at the edges of her consciousness.

"Please, don't leave me!"

"Trust yourself, Hazel," came the reply, as the glowing figure grew closer and more distinct. The symbol of a star beamed from the little girl's palm, like the north star on a dark night, drawing Hazel to her. "Together, we can overcome anything."

Closing the distance between them, Hazel's legs finally gave way and she stumbled into Bella's tiny outstretched arms. Their reunion was like the first breath of air after a long underwater dive, a lifeline that anchored them both in a world that seemed to slip away from their grasp. After everything they'd been through together, she'd grown to love the little girl.

"Thank goodness I found you here," Hazel whispered into Bella's shoulder, tears streaming down her face. "You need to tell me where you are in the real world, Bella, so the police can find you." Hazel's voice trembled as she held the girl firmly by the shoulders, her eyes never leaving Bella's. A surge of determination coursed through her veins, igniting her resolve like wildfire.

As Hazel kneeled down, gripping Bella's hands in hers, the little girl's spectral light flickered, her head shaking. "I don't know. H-He covers his face. It's dark." A tear rolled down Bella's cheek, sparkling like a diamond in the sun. "I want my daddy."

Bella looked over her shoulder as a noise echoed in the darkness, her body trembling. "We don't have much time, Hazel. There's something you need to know."

Pulling back slightly, Hazel looked into Bella's eyes, searching for answers. The urgency in Bella's expression was unmistakable; whatever she had to say, it was important. "What is it? What's happening?"

"New Orleans... the spirits are disappearing, fading away one by one. I don't know who took me or why, but they're draining my connection to the spirit world. They're using my power to fuel theirs."

The weight of Bella's words settled heavily on Hazel's shoulders, dread squeezing her windpipe. The city she had come to love, the people she had fought so hard to protect... Everything was at stake. But even more than that, the little girl who stood before her, someone who'd lost so much and had so much life left to live, was in mortal danger.

In that moment, the power they shared seemed to pulse between them, a tangible force that bound them together in their mission. They were stronger as one.

Hazel's shock and horror at Bella's abduction hung in the air like a heavy fog, her heart pounding in her chest. The spectral crisis plaguing New Orleans threatened to consume them all, and as she stared into Bella's eyes, she knew that time was running out.

Looking over Bella's shoulder as a sound echoed through the darkness again, Hazel pulled the little girl closer against her body. "Tell me everything you know. We need to understand what's happening to the spirits, and how it's connected to your abduction."

Bella nodded, her ethereal form shimmering. "They're coming, Hazel. You have to find me. The spirit world is in danger. Spirits are being taken into the darkness and it grows larger and darker every day. It spreads. It eats up all the energy of the remaining spirits and threatens to unravel the balance between our world and theirs."

As the dream shifted around them, the urgency of their situation pressed down upon Hazel like a leaden weight. Bella's form flickered, the glow surrounding her dimming slightly.

Pulling Bella tighter, Hazel wrapped her arms around the child's spectral form. Unlike the visions on the plane, where Bella looked just as she did in life, she appeared like nothing more than a specter, but her body was eerily solid. Hazel could feel the desperation emanating from Bella, and the weight of their mission settled heavily on her shoulders.

"Who's behind this?" Hazel asked, her voice barely above a whisper. "How do we stop them?"

"I don't know who's responsible," Bella admitted, her voice barely over a whisper. "But I do know that the void is growing stronger with each passing moment, feeding off the despair and hopelessness of the lost spirits. If we don't act soon, both worlds will be plunged into darkness. But Hazel..." When Bella pulled away and looked up, the expression in the little girl's eyes threatened to crush Hazel's heart. "Hazel, I tried to get out b-but I can't. I don't know how. You have to stop him. I want to go home."

"Then we'll find a way to close the void." Hazel's voice was sure, her gaze never wavering from Bella's face. Even though she felt just as helpless as a child, she was an adult, so she had to put on a brave face for Bella. "We'll save the spirits and bring you back where you belong. Together. And once you're safe, we'll go for ice cream, and you can get two scoops if you want."

"Yay!" Bella smiled, wrapping her arms around Hazel and hugging her again. "I know you can do it, but you have to hurry. Our connection won't last much longer."

Hazel nodded, her resolve hardening like steel. With every fiber of her being, she vowed to save Bella and the spirits of New Orleans, no matter the cost. As their connection began to fade, she clung to the memory of Bella's strength and knowledge, using it to fuel her own determination.

With one final, aching look at Bella, Hazel felt herself being drawn back into the waking world.

Hazel's eyes snapped open, her breath coming in short gasps as she stared at the ceiling above her bed. The dream had been a vivid reminder of the task that lay ahead, and the stakes had never been higher. Still, she didn't know where to start, especially when her stomach churned with nausea, forcing her onto her feet and into the bathroom.

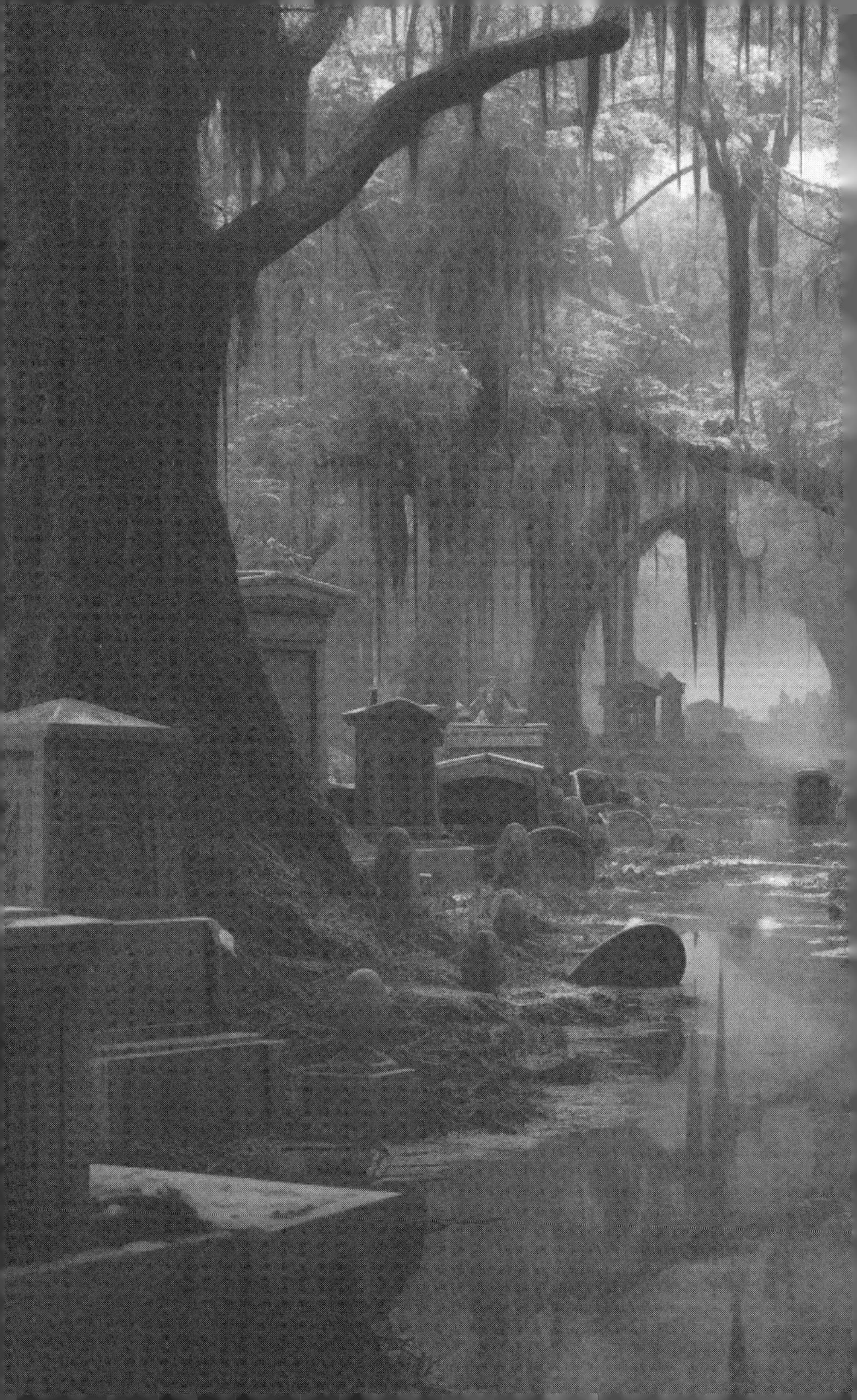

Chapter Nine
An Ordinary Girl with Extraordinary Visions

Surrounded by billowing clouds, Hazel's body was weightless as she floated through the hazy mist. In the distance, she could make out the faint roar of engines and glimpsed the shiny metal of an airplane emerging from the clouds. Beside her floated Bella, her wispy form flickering like a mirage, her dark brown hair in pigtails with pink ribbons.

"We have to stop it," the little girl said, her voice echoing as if traveling through a long tunnel.

Hazel nodded, her chest tight with apprehension. Together, they propelled themselves forward, arms outstretched toward the approaching aircraft. Hazel strained with the effort, willing her ethereal fingers to make contact, to alter the plane's course in any way she could.

Oblivious to their presence, the plane maintained its heading. Soul sinking back to the ground—where the plane was sure to follow—Hazel shared a dismayed look with Bella.

"We're too late," Bella cried, her anguish piercing Hazel's heart.

Jolting awake, Hazel's chest heaved, sheets tangling around her legs. Morning light filtered through the curtains of her bedroom, the familiar surroundings a stark contrast to the vivid dreamscape. She raked both hands through her tousled hair, trying to slow her rapid breaths. The same frustrating, hopeless nightmare had been plaguing her for months and all she wanted was for it to end. She'd been helpless to prevent the crash and people had died because of it. There was nothing to gain in her being further haunted by the memory of it, especially not when she had bigger problems to deal with. One, in particular, was the reason she'd spent the past two days in bed. *Morning sickness.*

Hazel sat up in bed, pressing her palms against her eyes until bursts of color dotted her vision. A headache was already building behind her temples, the intense dreams always leaving her more drained than the life inside her belly already did.

Swinging her legs over the side of the bed, she winced as her feet hit the cold floor. Sliding her feet into slippers, she shuffled to the bathroom, avoiding her reflection in the mirror and splashed water on her face. The cool liquid helped ground her, washing away the last wisps of the dream, but the sense of failure still clung to her, weighing on her heart. She and Bella had been so close, their hands outstretched, focused on diverting the aircraft's path. Yet despite their efforts—despite their foresight—the plane had crashed in a burst of flames and billowing smoke—killing everyone on board. *Just like it had in real life months ago.*

Hazel gripped the sides of the sink, anger and helplessness warring within her. When she'd received warnings about the crash in New Mexico, she was supposed to prevent the crash. She was supposed to be able to change the course of events. That was what her abilities were for, but she'd failed.

Instead, she was as useless as always, just an ordinary girl with extraordinary visions she couldn't control—extraordinary visions she couldn't decipher well enough to know what to do with the information. She couldn't use the things she saw in her visions to help people, not often enough to make it count.

With a frustrated sigh, she pushed off the sink and headed out of her and Tate's suite, hoping putting food in her system would help clear the fog from her mind and the nausea from her stomach. She had to pull it together. Bella was depending on her, even if she didn't fully understand how to help the missing child yet.

As Hazel stared down at her morning coffee, the rising steam did little to warm the chill creeping over her. Her usual light dimmed, Candy sat across from her, the space beside her empty. Jake was still missing. No matter how hard she tried, Candy could no longer feel even an ounce of his energy. There was still a chance he would reappear, but there was a sick feeling inside Hazel's chest telling her that he was another spirit gone without a trace, vanished into the dark void that had swallowed so many others these past few weeks. Either way, their actions wouldn't change. They had to find the missing spirits, and the missing little girl.

"You have to let me go with you, doll. I have to look for him."

Even though she understood the reasoning, Candy's words still sank Hazel's heart. After everything Candy and Jake had gone through, traversing life and death to be together, she knew she couldn't tell her friend no, but allowing Candy to leave their home and the fragile protections they had set up there would only put Candy at risk of being taken as well. Losing Candy was one thing she couldn't handle.

Setting her mug down, Hazel turned her eyes up to look at her friend. Candy's usual flair was subdued, her eyes red-rimmed from crying. "I can't take a chance of losing you too, Candy. Once you leave this house, I have no way of protecting you. I have no way of preventing you from being taken."

Candy shook her head, her energy flickering with her agitation. "It's not your job to keep me safe, Hazel. If anything, it's my job to keep you safe." A spectral tear slid down Candy's cheek, sparkling like a diamond in the sunlight streaming through the window until it disappeared into thin air. "My life is already over, doll. We don't know where the spirits are vanishing to, but if I were to disappear, it wouldn't be the same as if you went out there and died. There is no way I would ever let you go out there and face down something supernatural without me by your side. Tate can protect you from a lot, but he can't protect you from this. I can. I'm strong."

Reaching across the table, Hazel took Candy's hand in hers, giving it a gentle squeeze. "I know you're strong, Candy, but I can't bear the thought of losing you too. You're my best friend, my family. If anything happened to you, I don't know what I would do."

Candy's eyes softened, understanding passing between them. "I know, but we're in this together. We've always been in this together. I'm not going to let you face this alone."

Hazel nodded, the weight of Candy's words settling in her chest. She couldn't do this alone, not with the stakes so high. She needed Candy by her side, no matter the risk. "Alright. But we have to be careful. We don't know what we're up against, or what's happening to these spirits. And I have to call Tate. Just because he can't help with the supernatural stuff doesn't mean he can't help at all. After everything we've been through, he needs to know our next moves."

Candy smiled, the flicker of light returning to her eyes. "I know, and that's a good plan. It's never a bad idea to have your beefcake husband watching our backs." Although a smirk twisted the side of Candy's lips, Hazel knew better than to think her friend was taking the situation lightly. "We'll be extra careful. We'll look out for each other. We'll be okay."

Candy's unwavering loyalty warmed Hazel's heart, and she couldn't help but smile. They would track down Bella and Jake. They would uncover the truth behind the strange disappearances, no matter the cost. Even so, there was a feeling of unease beneath the surface. There was so much she didn't know and the stakes were too high to jump into the case half-cocked like she usually did. If she handled this case as she'd handled so many others, more than one child would be lost.

*

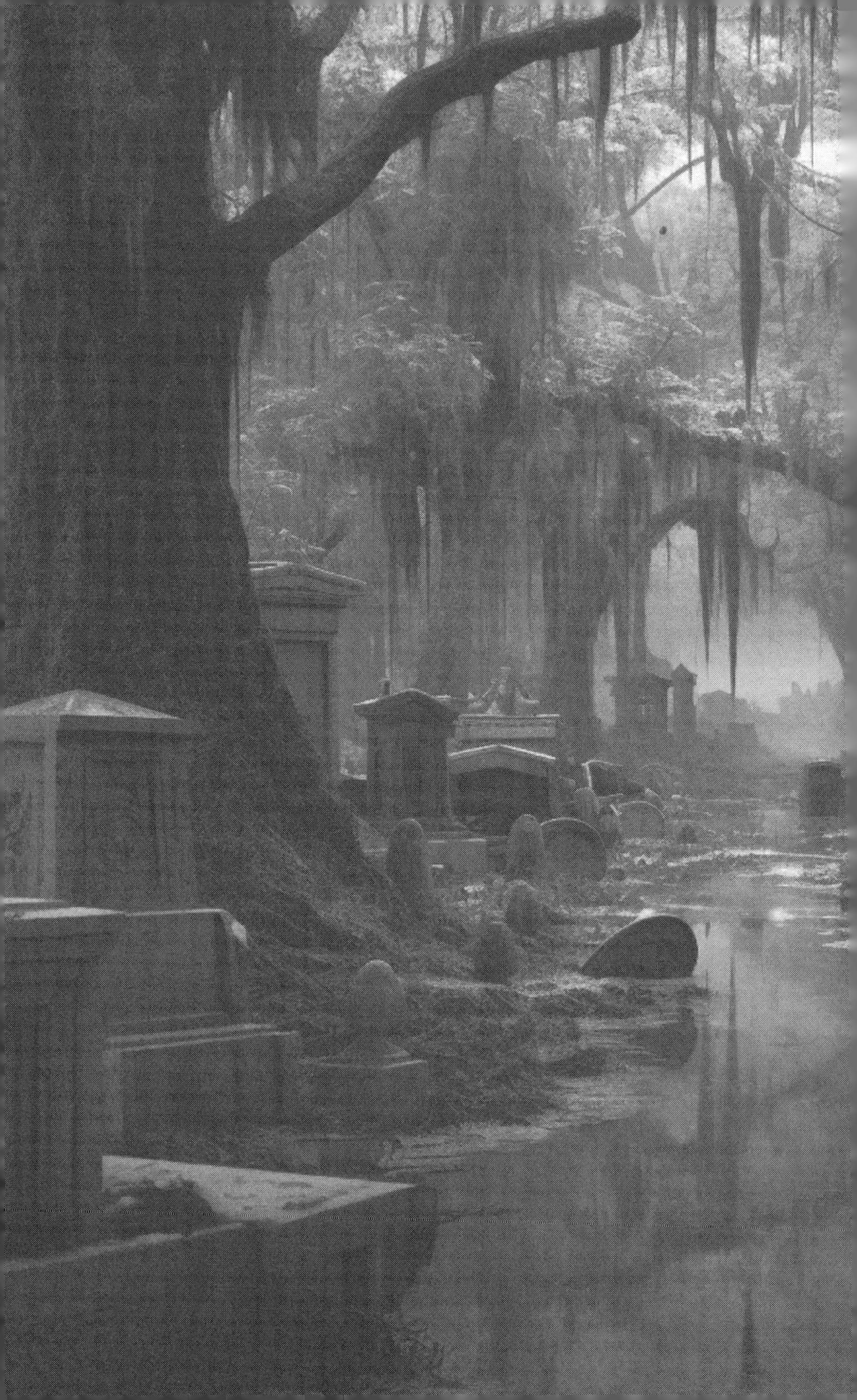

Chapter Ten
The Ghostly Underworld

Hazel's boots clicked against the stone walkway leading to the front of Celeste's cottage. The fall breeze made the many wind chimes jingle, only making Celeste's storybook cottage feel more magical. Pausing at the steps to the front porch, she turned to look at the wildflowers scattered across the property, breathing in deeply. Even with Candy floating beside her, nervousness twisted in Hazel's stomach. She needed Celeste's help, needed the ancient wisdom the woman possessed if she had any hope of navigating the perilous ghostly underworld and figuring out what was going on. Aside from Celeste and her mother, she didn't know who else to turn to, and her mother was across the country.

"Are you afraid she's going to cut your hair again?"

Shivers raced up Hazel's cheek as Candy tousled her hair, but she still huffed a laugh.

"Ha ha. Not funny."

Hesitating for only another second, she smoothed her sweaty palms over her jeans and strode up the front steps, raising her fist to knock on the purple front door. It didn't take long for the door to swing inward, Celeste's slender silhouette stepping into frame.

"Hazel." The elderly Wiccan's wizened face creased into a smile, her waist-length blond hair twisted into a braid and draped over her shoulder. "Come in, come in. I'll put on some tea."

Sharing a glance with Candy, Hazel nodded, following Celeste inside.

The scent of incense thickened as Celeste led her down a short hallway that was lined with bookcases crammed full of leather-bound tomes and curious artifacts, mingling with dried herbs and smoke. They emerged into the small tea room, every surface draped in embroidered scarves, more artifacts stored on every shelf and in every cabinet.

Disappearing into the kitchen, Celeste returned a moment later with the tea tray, settling onto an overstuffed velvet armchair and setting the tray on a small table. Hazel perched on the chair beside her, back rigid. From the corner of her eye, she watched as Candy nosed around in Celeste's things, her own gaze taking in the crystals dangling from the ceiling and animal skulls adorning the shelves. She'd been there a few times already, but there always seemed to be something new to look at.

"Well now," Celeste said, taking a sip of her tea. "Tell me what brings you to my door today."

Meeting the older woman's eyes, Hazel took a steadying breath, unsure what to ask for. "Since we've spoken last, my best friend, Candy, the man she loves disappeared, and the child, Bella, is still missing as well. I'm no closer to finding either of them and I don't think the police are any closer to finding Bella either." Bile burning up Hazel's throat, she took a sip of her tea, taking a moment to continue. "I just don't know where to start. I am so out of my depths."

Celeste nodded, her expression grave. "The ghostly underworld is not a place for the faint of heart, but you're stronger than you think, Hazel, and the child in your womb brings you more strength, not less."

A chill traced its way up Hazel's spine at Celeste's words. She had never mentioned being pregnant to the older woman. Taking another sip of her tea, Hazel released a shaky breath.

"What do I need to do?"

Celeste's eyes flicked up as Candy lowered herself onto the arm of Hazel's chair, before turning her gaze back to Hazel's.

"The ghostly underworld exists as a parallel realm to our own. It is a shadowy in-between filled with spirits unable to move on–ghosts, wraiths, specters. Portals connect our world to theirs, allowing passage between the realms."

Hazel's pulse quickened as she absorbed Celeste's words. Being able to help spirits cross over had been passed down in her family for generations, but she'd never known where the spirits went once they left the land of the living, and the thought of descending into their domain was terrifying.

"Like any journey to a foreign land, you must take certain precautions. Protection spells to shield your spirit, sacred herbs to ward off malevolent entities. I will provide you with all you require."

Hazel moistened her dry lips. "And the necromancer? Or whoever is doing this? How can I defeat them and free Bella and the spirits?"

"Trust in your abilities," Celeste said, reaching forward and taking Hazel's hand. "You have gifts, Hazel, even if you don't realize it. Together we will hone them into weapons."

In spite of her fear, Hazel met Celeste's intense gaze, resolve flowing through her. With Celeste as her mentor, she would brave the ghostly underworld. She didn't see any other way.

Rising from her chair, Celeste beckoned for Hazel to follow her as she walked down the hall and into a room glowing with candlelight. The shelves lining the walls overflowed with jars of herbs, vials of oils, bundles of sage and sweetgrass. There was a low altar against one wall, holding crystals, feathers, and bones. Hazel inhaled the heady scents as Celeste busied herself gathering ingredients.

"For protection," Celeste murmured, measuring out herbs into a mortar. "Mugwort, to ward off evil. Rosemary, for mental clarity." Adding drops of oil, Celeste ground the mixture into a fine paste as Hazel watched.

"This amulet will shield your spirit." She looped a leather cord through a polished stone and placed it around Hazel's neck, the smooth stone against Hazel's skin reminding her of the sapphire necklace she helped Angela find all those months before.

With the herbal paste in her hand, Celeste pressed it into Hazel's temples, forehead, and wrists. "Mark yourself with this before entering any portal. It should disguise you from those who mean harm."

Watching closely, Hazel committed each step to memory. With no experience in the practice of Wicca, she didn't know how any of it worked, or *if* it worked at all, but with no other options, she had to try.

Hazel took a deep breath as Celeste led her into the back room. The curtains were drawn, casting the space in shadow. A ring of candles flickering around a large mirror leaning against the far wall was the only light in the room.

"This is a portal," Celeste said, guiding Hazel to kneel before it, "to the realm between worlds."

Holding the amulet at her neck, Hazel shivered, trying to draw courage from its protective power. The portal exuded an energy that raised the hairs on her arms.

Celeste turned to her, expression serious. "Remember, the ghostly plane can disorient even the most experienced traveler. Keep your wits about you."

Hazel nodded, her mouth dry, her stomach turning. Behind Celeste, Candy's face was twisted with worry, but she didn't intervene. They both knew Hazel had to do this.

"You may encounter entities that will try to deceive you, or spirits that have forgotten they have passed on." Celeste gripped Hazel's shoulders. "Trust your instincts if anything feels amiss. If you lose your way, focus on my voice calling you back."

Eyes flicking up to look at her friend again, Hazel swallowed hard. "I won't fail."

Candy moved toward her, wrapping her in a hug. "Be careful, doll. Come back to us or I'm going to go in after you."

Tears burning the backs of Hazel's eyes, she nodded, turning her gaze back to Celeste. Even as she tried to ready herself to go into the spiritual realm, her instincts told her to run away—to go home to her husband and never look back.

Celeste squeezed her arm, pulling her attention back to her reality. "Trust in your gifts. And return before the sun rises, while the veil is thin."

With a final steadying breath, Hazel leaned toward the mirror. Its surface shimmered, ready to deliver her into the unknown.

With everything in place, and Candy by her side, Celeste led Hazel through chanting an incantation, their voices weaving together in the candlelit room. The words were foreign, yet resonated deep within Hazel. She could feel power thrumming just beneath her skin.

When the chant ended, Celeste grasped Hazel's hands. "You have all you need now, dear. Trust in yourself."

The portal surface parted like water as Hazel touched the glass. Heart pounding, she slipped into the ghostly underworld.

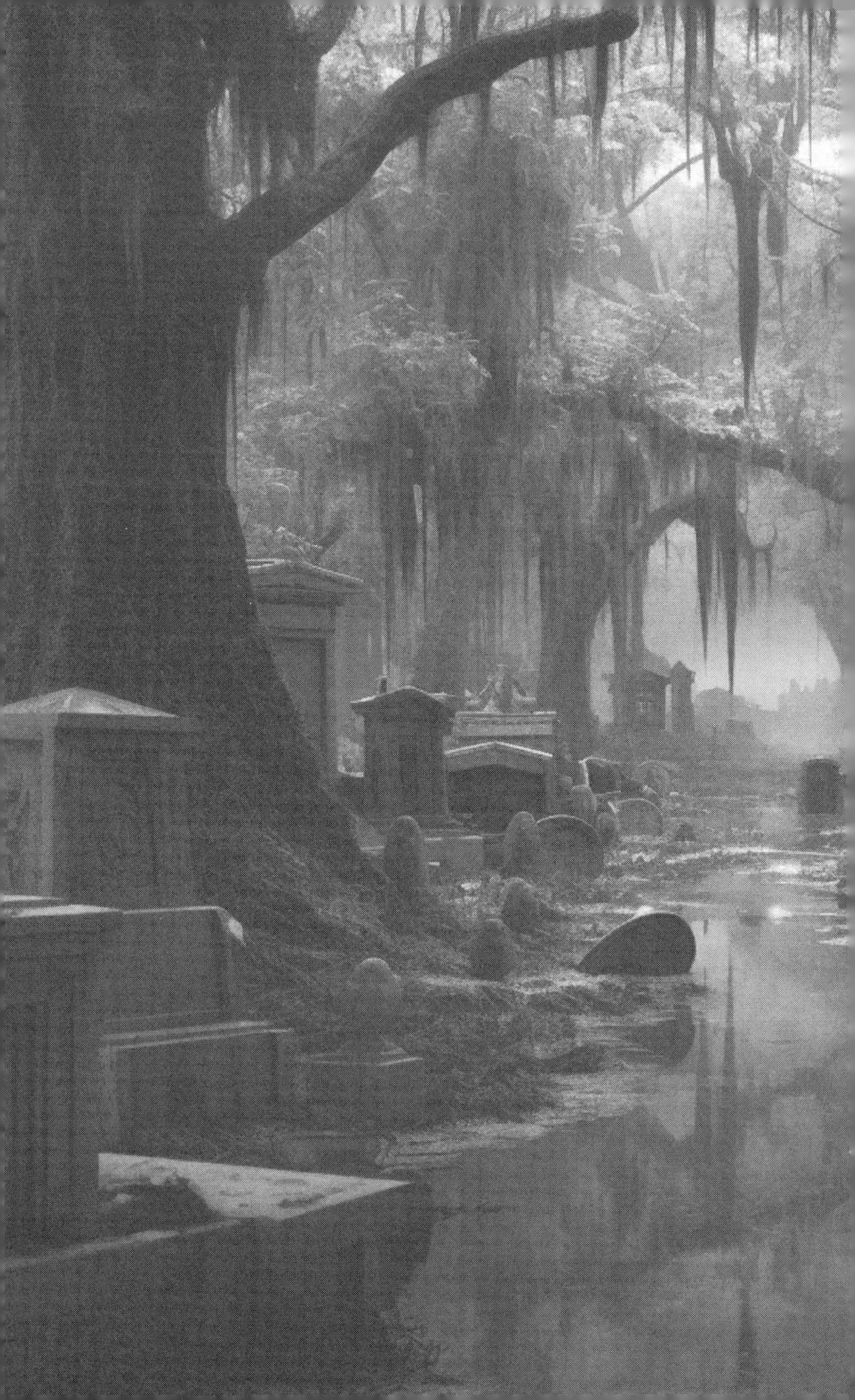

Chapter Eleven
The Crone, The Spirit, & The Raven

Wisps of fog drifted over barren ground and dead trees with gnarled branches when Hazel found herself standing in a gray, muted landscape. In the distance, shadowy figures wandered, too far away to make out any features.

Hazel suppressed a shiver, her senses on high alert as she made her way deeper into the misty realm. The atmosphere grew heavier, weighed down by the sorrow and unrest of souls unable to move on.

A whisper of movement caught her attention and Hazel turned, peering into the gloom just in time to see a shape dart behind a twisted tree, too quick to make out.

"Hello?"

A raspy chuckle answered a heartbeat before the shape glided out, features forming into the translucent figure of a gangly young man. One side of his face was badly scarred, his hair falling in matted locks over his eyes.

"Well met, mortal," he greeted with a mocking bow. "You're a long way from home."

Hazel inclined her head, unsure who she could trust or who to talk to. "I'm searching for someone...a young living girl. Have you seen her?"

The spirit's eyes glinted. "I might know something...for a price."

Realizing he intended on playing games with her, Hazel frowned and pulled a small crystal from her bag, offering it to the spirit. A gift for the dead, to entice cooperation. He didn't hesitate to take it.

"Her name—Bella?" He peered down at her, scratching the air where his chin should have been. "Strong magic in that one. But magic can't save her from those determined to use it. Heed the raven's flight...and follow the stars."

With the cryptic warning, he vanished, leaving Hazel to ponder his words as she continued her search. Raven's flight and follow stars...she would decipher his clue. She had to, for Bella's sake.

Hazel pressed on through the shadowed forest, leaves and mist swirling around her. In the distance, a raven cawed, its cry echoing strangely among the trees.

She followed the sound until she reached a small glen, her boots silent on the mossy ground. Ahead, a glowing figure sat upon a fallen log, humming just over the wind.

"Hello?"

"Welcome, child." Looking up, the spirit's gentle face was framed by long, flowing hair, her voice musical. "I am Amelia. Are you lost?"

Hazel nodded, the entire situation starting to feel like one of her dreams in the darkness. "I'm looking for someone—a young living girl named Bella. She's been taken. Have you seen her?"

A knowing look passed across Amelia's pale eyes. "Ah yes, taken by the dark one. His lair lies deep within the forest, but tread carefully, young one. His minions guard the path."

Even with the warning, Hazel felt a spark of hope. "Can you show me the way?"

With a shake of Amelia's head, Hazel's spark of hope vanished. "I cannot go nearer to that evil place, but I can give you this."

Reaching forward, the spirit pressed a smooth stone into Hazel's hand, ancient runes glowing across its surface. Hazel had never seen anything like it, but she could sense the power surging within it.

"For protection," Amelia whispered. "Now go, and stay true to your quest."

Hazel nodded, moving deeper into the shadowy forest, following the path Amelia had indicated. An unnatural hush fell over the woods, broken only by the occasional snap of a twig under her boots. She paused, listening as the whispers of spirits echoed in the distance, their pain setting her teeth on edge.

Even though she saw no one, and even with her fingers closed around the smooth stone Amelia had given her for protection, her senses remained on high alert. In such a dark place, danger lurked in the shadows.

A raspy cackle sounded from somewhere to Hazel's right, a shape darting behind a tree. Hazel's pulse quickened, fear tightening her chest and making it hard to breathe.

"I know you're there," she called out, trying to slow her breathing. "Show yourself!"

Another grating laugh answered. A shadowy figure crept from the underbrush, its face obscured by a dark cowl, its bony fingers tipped with crooked claws.

The crone circled Hazel, her eyes glowing crimson. "You're far from home, little lamb," she croaked. "These woods belong to the spirits. You shouldn't have come here unless you want to become one too."

Skin crawling like thousands of tiny spiders covered her, Hazel wrapped her hand around the stone Amelia had given her, swallowing back her fear. "I'm looking for my friend. Step aside and I'll be on my way."

The crone bared her rotten teeth. "No one leaves this forest, little lamb!"

Squeezing the stone, Hazel stepped to the side, letting the crone stumble past. As the creature spun back around, the stone in Hazel's hand surged with a blinding light, engulfing the crone and turning her into vapor, her anguished wail echoing through the forest.

Watching the empty space where the creature had stood, Hazel dropped the stone to the ground, trying to catch her breath. All the time she'd spent in the darkness—in the dreams and memories that weren't her own—she'd never experienced anything like what she was going through at that moment.

Blowing out a breath, Hazel picked the stone back up from the ground and tucked it in her pocket, heading deeper into the mist-shrouded forest, senses alert for any sign of danger. The contorted trees seemed to lean in around her, their twisted branches like bony fingers grasping at the air. Somewhere an owl hooted, the lonely sound echoing through the stillness.

Hazel shivered, pulling her jacket tighter. Although visions of spirits flickered in the distance, she didn't trust any of them for guidance, which left her completely lost. Aside from Bella and Jake, she didn't know what she was looking for, nor did she know if the spirits in the forest were those who were missing from New Orleans. Something told her they weren't, and that the spirits she was looking for were somewhere else altogether.

The air around her was silent enough to hear her panting breath, when a twig snapped behind her. Hazel spun, hand flying to the stone in her pocket. The figure of a man emerged from the trees, flickering like a dying candle, translucent and solemn-faced. His old-fashioned clothes were tattered, and a rusted sword hung at his side.

Halting her steps, Hazel stood ready to defend herself, but the spirit made no move to attack. Instead, his head tilted to the side like a curious puppy.

"You do not belong here, mortal," he said, voice hollow. "These woods hold only peril."

Chancing a step forward, Hazel slid the stone back in her pocket. "What's your name?"

The ghost was silent for a long moment. Then his head straightened and he leaned forward in a bow. "Charles Lafayette Senior, at your service, Madame." When his dark eyes met hers again, his expression turned serious. "I know the dark mage you seek, but his power is great. I can lead you to where you can find answers, but cannot aid you further."

Wary but hopeful, Hazel gestured for him to show the way. With no other options, she had to trust him, hoping he would lead her to salvation and not to ruin.

For what seemed like miles, the ghost drifted through the dark forest, Hazel close behind. She kept her head on a swivel, ready to defend herself if he was leading her into a trap, but he glided ahead in silence, showing no signs of hostility.

After some time, they came to a large stone wall. Although the spirit passed through as though it wasn't there, Hazel had to feel along the stone, looking for a hidden entrance. When she'd nearly given up hope, her fingers caught on a crevice, and a section of the stone slid away at her touch, revealing a passage.

With one hand on her amulet, she followed behind Charles as he floated down the stairs and into the darkness beyond. The further down they descended, the colder it became, the stone walls dripping with icy condensation.

At the bottom of the eerie staircase was a vast chamber filled with ancient artifacts—staffs, spellbooks, jars of preserved creatures floating in sickly green liquid, and in the center was a table holding an expansive map marked with strange symbols.

Hazel moved closer, eyes tracing the map's markings. There were locations labeled with notes, both in English and in languages she didn't recognize, as well as doodles of various shapes and creatures, but one symbol stood out—a star enclosed in a circle. The same mark that was on Bella's palm.

Suddenly it dawned on her. "Her power." The air around her chilling, Hazel could see her breath as she exhaled. "He plans to use it to open the gateways between worlds."

Hazel's mind raced, her attention so caught up on what was in front of her that she barely noticed the trap she'd walked into. Metal hinges squealed and Hazel whirled around as the heavy wooden door slammed closed, sealing her in the chamber. From the shadows emerged three wraith-like figures, their ghostly forms flickering in the dim light.

"You cannot stop what has already begun," one wraith hissed, its voice like nails on a chalkboard.

Her mind immediately went to her family—to Tate, Candy, and the baby in her womb as she stood her ground, her hand tightening on the amulet.

Closing her eyes, she murmured the only other incantation Celeste taught her, one to banish evil spirits, channeling her energy into the amulet.

The wraiths shrieked and advanced on her, but Hazel held fast, the amulet flaring with light. With a final pulse, the wraiths dissolved into wisps of darkness.

With the wraiths gone, the door opened with ease, allowing her to leave the room.

Wasting no time, she rushed back up the stairs as fast as she could. She knew why the necromancer had taken Bella. She realized all that mattered, as she burst out of the underground chamber and back into the gloomy supernatural realm, was finding Bella before the necromancer could use her gift to unleash peril upon both the living and the dead.

Heart pounding hard enough to make her dizzy, Hazel paused for only a moment to get her bearings, consulting the newly discovered map still clutched in her hand. With the wraiths discorporated behind her, she had a head start, but she knew others would soon be on her trail. She had to make it back to the mortal plane to warn the others about the grave peril Bella was in. The girl's rare power over the dead made her the key to a far more destructive outcome than they could have ever imagined—a sort of spirit apocalypse.

Hazel broke into a run, her boots echoing on the leaf-littered ground as she navigated through the shadowy spirit world. Wisps fluttered by her, whispering an ominous tune in her wake. The air grew colder, raising the hairs on the back of her neck, telling her she was being followed, but she didn't slow down.

Glancing over her shoulder, three shadowy specters drifted after her, their smoky forms coiling and writhing. With the glimmer of the portal up ahead, she picked up her speed, clutching her amulet as she aimed straight for the way out. The sound of the specters' unearthly moans grew louder, spurring Hazel onward.

With a final burst of effort, she leapt through the portal, a zing of electricity passing through her as she passed back into the mortal realm. Before her eyes fluttered open, she felt the portal close behind her telling her she was safe, but only for the moment. There was no time to waste if she wanted to stay that way.

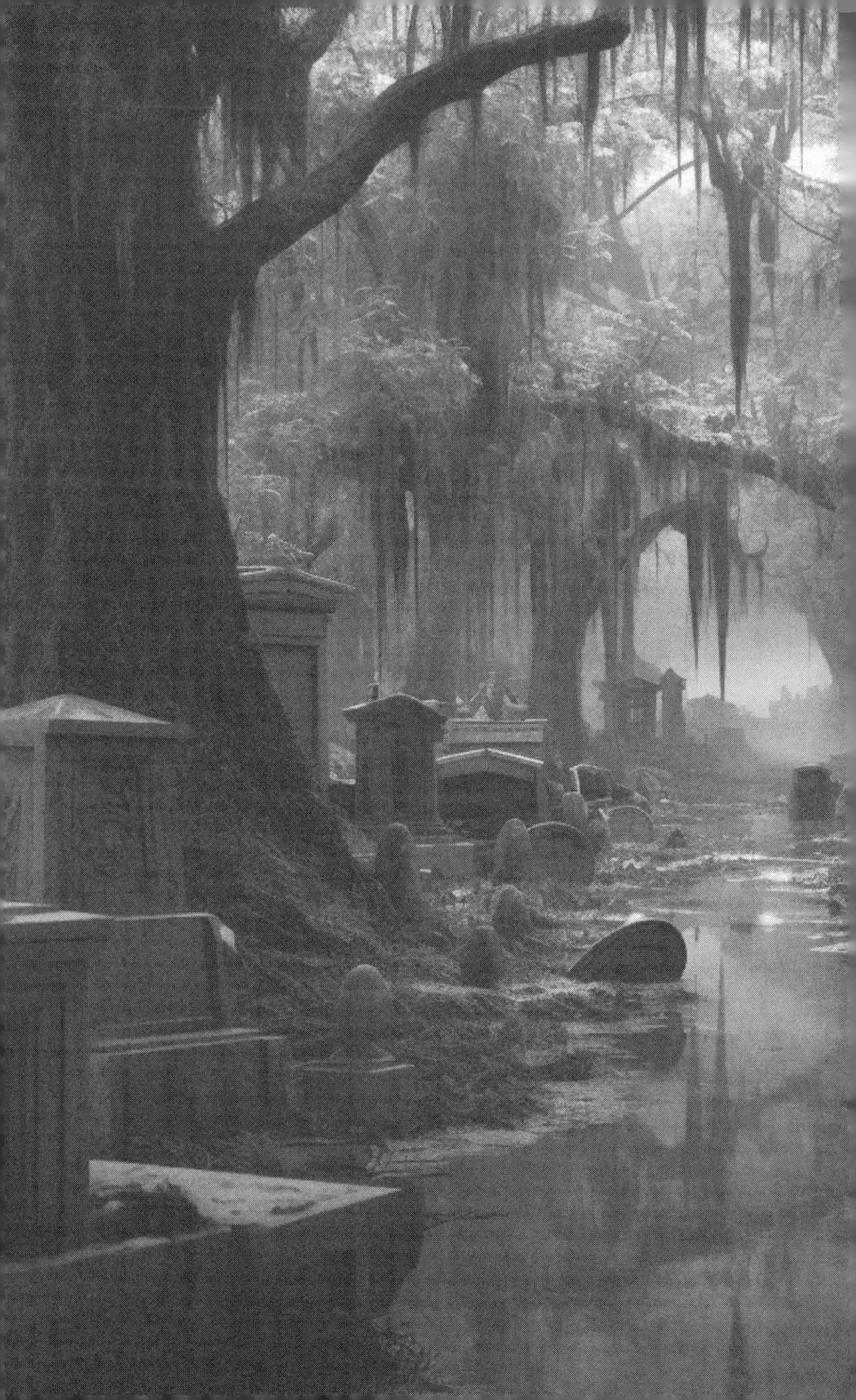

Chapter Twelve
A Little R & R

Stumbling through the garage door after driving home from Celeste's cottage, the weight of exhaustion pulled at Hazel's limbs. The journey into the spirit realm had drained every ounce of energy from her body. Before she even opened the door, Tate was in the doorway, his strong arms wrapping around her as she sagged against him.

"Hey, I've got you." Brushing a stray hair from her face, his eyes were dark with concern. "Are you okay?"

Hazel offered a weak smile. "I'm fine, just tired." She knew she must look a mess—clothes rumpled, hair wild—but Tate's embrace was warm and comforting, his body sturdy against her own, and he loved her for who she was.

Keeping an arm around her shoulders, he led her to the living room, tension leaving her body with every step. "Let's get you settled on the couch."

Hazel sank onto the soft cushions, leaning her head back and closing her eyes. The couch dipped as Tate sat beside her and reached for her hand, their fingers intertwining.

"Do you want to talk about it?"

Snuggling into his side, she cracked one eye open. "Not really. It was...intense. I learned some things, but..." She shuddered. "I don't want to think about it right now."

Never one to push her, Tate nodded, squeezing her hand. "Whenever you're ready."

As they sat in silence for a few moments, the quiet of the house settled over Hazel. She focused on the warmth of Tate's hand in hers, grounding her. She was home. She was safe. Whatever they would face next, at least they would face it together.

Resting her head on Tate's shoulder, she let her body relax against his, taking comfort in his familiar scent. His arm came around her, his hand stroking her hair.

"I'm glad you're home," she murmured against his chest, drawing in a deep breath as she listened to his heart beat against her ear.

Tate pressed a kiss to the top of her head. "There's nowhere else I'd rather be."

As they held each other, the stresses of the day slowly ebbed away. Hazel's eyelids grew heavy, lulled by Tate's steady heartbeat under her ear.

She was just drifting off when a flash of red in her peripheral vision made her tense, but it was only Candy, materializing in the armchair across from them. Her fiery hair seemed to glow in the low light.

"Hey, doll." With a sad smile, Candy tucked her legs under her. "Sorry I'm late."

Hazel sat up straighter, shaking off her drowsiness. "Candy. I was starting to worry..."

"I know. I'm sorry." Even as Hazel stared at her, Candy's form flickered. "I just needed time to recharge after today, but I'm here now."

Hazel nodded, knowing they still had a lot to discuss and plans to make, but that could wait till morning. For that moment, it was enough just having her best friend close again.

"Get some rest," Candy said, curling up on her chair and turning to look at the television. "We'll figure this out together."

With Jake gone, Hazel didn't want to push. She knew Candy was worried, that her best friend was devastated, and that she was probably just as overwhelmed as Hazel was. Settling back against Tate, she let out a sigh. What mattered was that they were together. She let her eyes fall closed once more, comforted by the two people she loved most in the world, one on either side of her. When she felt better, she intended to check in with her mother and get an update on her father, but for the time being, all she wanted to do was recuperate.

Hazel's moment of peace was short-lived. No sooner had she started to drift off again than her stomach roiled, that now too-familiar wave of nausea hitting her hard.

Groaning, she bolted upright, one hand flying to her mouth. Candy was at her side in an instant, Tate darting off into the kitchen. "Oh, doll. Morning sickness again?"

All Hazel could do was nod, not trusting herself to open her mouth. It had gone from morning sickness to all-day sickness.

"Here." Returning to his place beside her, Tate pressed a cool, wet cloth against her face.

Hazel clutched it, willing her rebelling stomach to settle. The constant queasiness made everything else ten times harder, sapping her energy when she needed it most. She was struggling enough as it was to hone her powers, to ready herself for the fight ahead. Growing a life inside of her and being responsible for that life, on top of everything else, was just hard. It was just hard.

"Just breathe," Tate said, his strong hand rubbing gentle circles on her back. "It'll pass."

After a few agonizing minutes, Hazel sagged against him in relief when the worst of the nausea finally began to ebb.

"I'm so over this," she breathed, hating the words as they left her lips.

Nuzzling against Tate's chest, she placed her hand on his stomach, grateful to have him by her side. "How am I supposed to save the world when I can barely make it through the day without puking?"

Candy gave her a sympathetic look from where she floated in the middle of the room. "I know it's hard, but you're strong, baby bird. Stronger than anyone I've ever known. You can do this."

Although she wasn't feeling very confident at that moment, Hazel managed a small smile. However lost she felt, Candy always knew exactly what to say, and Tate's unwavering support helped anchor her too.

Taking a deep breath, Hazel tried to steal herself. They would get through everything together, one day at a time.

Tate's fingers trailed up and down her arms, his touch soothing. "You're doing great. I know it doesn't feel like it, but you are. And we're here for you, every step of the way."

Tilting her head back, Hazel looked up at him, struck by the tenderness in his blue eyes. No matter how bleak things seemed, he always saw the best in her and believed in her, even when she doubted herself.

She reached up, fingers brushing his stubbled jaw, and he turned his head to press a kiss to her palm. The contact sent a spark skittering through her, momentarily chasing away the nausea.

It had been too long since they'd had any real time alone together, since she'd let herself get lost in his arms, his kisses, the solid strength of his body. She needed that connection—that reminder he was real and there with her. What she needed in that moment was to be touched, *desired*. To feel like herself again, instead of just the girl with the supernatural destiny looming over her.

Curling her fingers into his shirt, she tugged him down, pressing her lips to his. With every swipe of Tate's tongue, the familiar taste and heat of him began to thaw the chill of fear paralyzing her insides, replacing that fear with the heat of desire. In the corner of her eye, she saw Candy disapparate, leaving them alone.

Deepening the kiss, Tate's hands slid under her thighs, lifting her until she was straddling his lap and carrying her into their bedroom, kicking the door closed behind them.

The light from the moon fell in beams through the window, illuminating their room in its glowing blue light. Hazel's heart fluttered with anticipation as Tate laid her down on the bed, his gaze smoldering as he looked down at her. His touch was gentle but filled with a longing that made her skin quiver. Pulling him close, her breath hitched, heat pooling low in her stomach as he settled between her thighs, his hardness pressing against her center.

The feel of his lips was like liquid fire on hers, spreading flames through every inch of her body and making it ache for more. She ran her hands over his back, savoring the feel of his muscular frame beneath her fingertips. Her head fell back, lost in pleasure when Tate's mouth left hers to trail kisses down her neck. The nausea was already a distant memory.

All that mattered was his hands and lips worshiping her body, making her feel beautiful, cherished, reminding her that she was still human too. She was still a woman who needed to be loved and not just someone who was responsible for things she didn't understand.

As their clothes fell away and their bodies joined in the throes of passion, Hazel let everything else slip away. The spirits, the necromancer, all of it faded into the background.

There was only Tate, his blue eyes burning into hers, his voice ragged in her ear. "I love you."

At that moment, it was enough.

Her body pleasantly sore and sated, Hazel drifted in a hazy state between sleep and waking. Tate's arm was a comforting weight across her waist, his breath stirring her hair. Smiling to herself, she snuggled closer to him, her eyelids growing heavy.

As she turned to look at the moonlight coming in through the window blinds, the darkness shifted. The familiar shapes of the bedroom faded, replaced by a vast, gloomy space. Hazel's dreams were dark and shapeless, swirling with mysterious shadows that threatened to consume her in their depths. Tensing, her senses went on high alert when she realized she wasn't in her bed anymore. She'd returned to the darkness.

An icy breeze chilled the air as she stood in the middle of a cavernous space, the air smelling stale, with an undertone of something sickly sweet and rotten. She walked in the direction her instincts pulled her, the waterlogged soil squishing beneath her bare feet. Although she couldn't make out details of her surroundings, shadows of structures stood out in the obscurity, like lifeless sentinels haunting the landscape.

Wrapping her arms around her chest, she peered into the void when a small sound caught her attention. Then, like a beacon of light in the darkness, seven-year-old Bella appeared before her. The little girl's eyes were wide and pleading, desperation etching into every line of her face. Unlike the times Hazel had seen Bella in their shared space before, the child's clothes were worn and dirty, fatigue dulling her eyes.

"Bella." Hazel took a step forward, reaching out her hand.

Hesitating only for a moment as she looked over her shoulder into the darkness, Bella placed her tiny hands into Hazel's, the star on her palm shining like it was made of flames. "Bella, are you okay?"

Curling into Hazel's body, Bella shook her head, her brown ponytail matted. "You have to find me, Hazel. He's hurting us."

The words wrenched Hazel's heart open, her legs collapsing under her until she was on her knees, looking into the seven-year-old's eyes. "I'm trying, Bella. Can you tell me where you are? Can you tell me anything?"

As Bella pulled away, she started to fade, her edges blurring. "Somewhere dark and made of stone. Please hurry!"

Panic rising in her throat, Hazel reached for Bella, but her hands passed right through the apparition.

"No, wait! I need more. How do I find you?"

Without another word, the ghostly girl was already gone, vanished back into the shadows, leaving Hazel alone again in the sinister darkness.

As though being sucked through a vacuum, Hazel jolted awake, her eyes shooting open. Early morning light filtered through the curtains. She was back in her own room, Tate still sleeping soundly beside her.

Pressing a hand to her racing heart, she struggled to slow her panicked breaths. The moments in the darkness had seemed so real. She could still smell the stench of rot, could still hear Bella's haunting voice. They were running out of time to find Bella and the other spirits, to stop the necromancer before he did something even more twisted with his unnatural powers.

The thought of the innocent little girl trapped in that nightmarish place made Hazel's stomach churn. After everything Bella had been through, after losing her mother in such an awful way and at such a young age, Hazel worried she may never recover. Bella needed to be home with her father, and, more than anything, she needed to learn how to control her powers so they didn't rule her life. At only seven–years-old, Bella had a lot of life left to live, and she deserved a chance at a normal life. They both did.

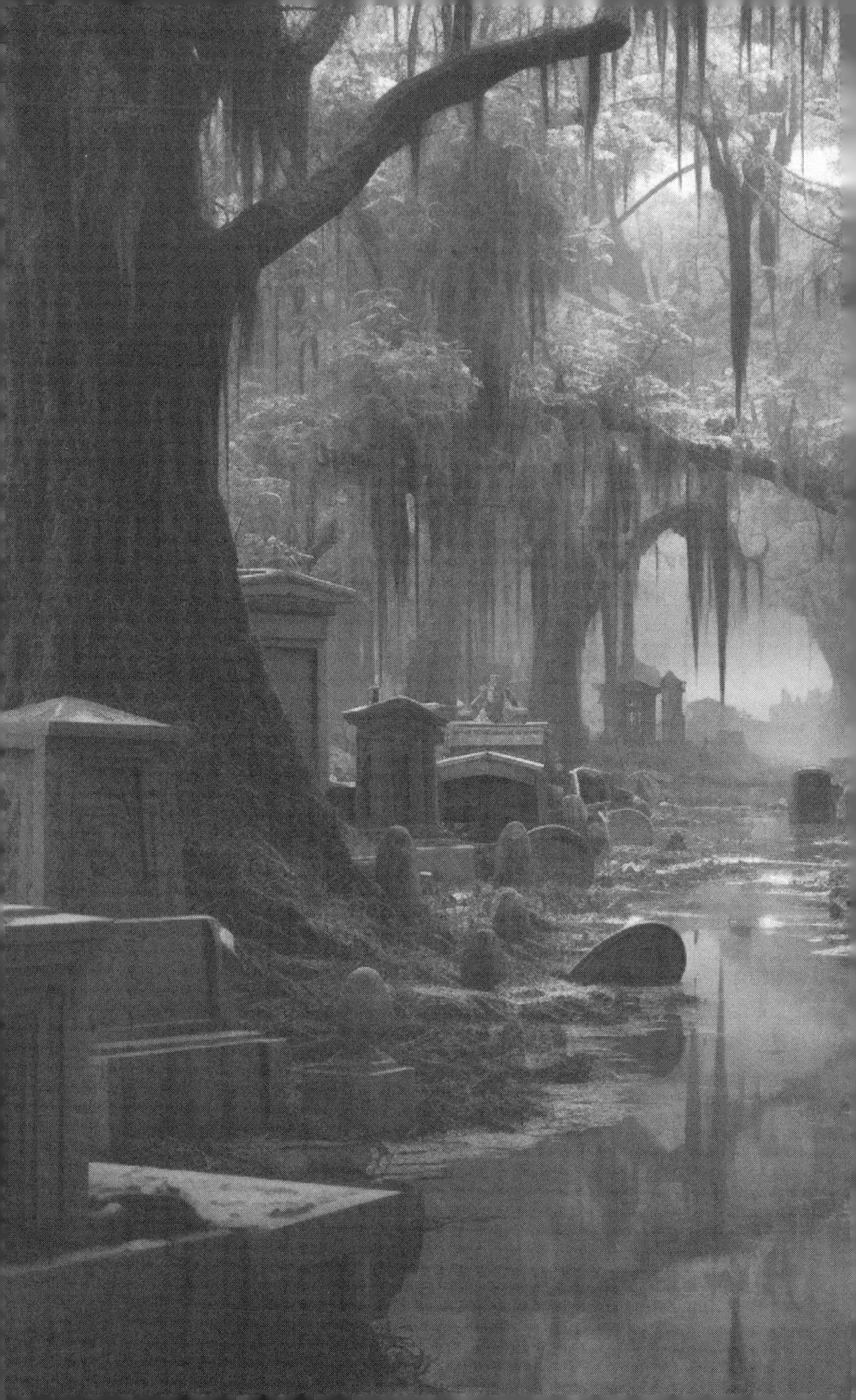

Chapter Thirteen
Friends and Allies

Taking a deep breath, Hazel slipped out of bed, careful not to disturb Tate, and stepped out of their bedroom.

Shuffling into the kitchen, she started a pot of coffee, hoping caffeine would sharpen her focus. She was just setting out mugs when Candy drifted into the room, her usual cheerful expression replaced by a more somber one.

"Rough night, doll?"

Hazel nodded, the nausea in her stomach telling her that coffee may not be a wise idea. "Bella came to me again. She's somewhere dark and dirty, but I don't know where. We have to find her, Candy."

As Candy moved to Hazel's side, she placed an icy hand on her shoulder, but the touch was reassuring. "We will, but you know we can't do this alone. We need help."

Tate shuffled into the kitchen a few minutes later, his hair adorably mussed from sleep. He took one look at Hazel's tense face and was instantly concerned.

"What's going on?"

As the two of them sipped their coffee, Hazel shared her dream with him, Tate's expression twisting as he listened to each detail. She also recounted her visit to the supernatural realm. Every detail felt significant. She knew there were parts of her gift that bothered him—the parts that put her in danger. However, a child was missing, and that made it a different situation altogether.

"We need a plan. There's too much ground to cover and not enough to go on, and with the police doing their own investigation..." Running his fingers through his hair, Tate stood to refill his coffee. "We need to keep Bourgeois abreast of what you're doing. We should talk to him again. See if his department has learned anything new in the past twenty four hours."

Candy nodded, slipping into the chair beside Hazel and leaning over the table, her chin resting on her palm. "The more manpower against this creep, the better."

The thought of running everything past the police department tightened Hazel's chest, filling her with unease. It just wasn't how she'd done things before, although she knew Tate was right. If she didn't have backup, the outcome could be disastrous. With a sigh, she met Tate's gaze and squeezed his hand.

"Alright. Let's call him."

A gust of wind whipped through the trees, sending a shiver down Hazel's spine as she sat with Tate on the front porch swing, waiting for Detective Bourgeois. There was tension and anxiety in the air, every second feeling like it was an eternity while they awaited news of Bella. There was a storm coming, and she was afraid it wasn't just a rain storm. Hazel clutched her sweater tightly around her, seeking warmth in more ways than one.

The rumble of an engine cut through the eerie silence, signaling his approach, just before his car pulled up to the curb. The detective dipped his chin as he climbed out of the car.

"Evening, Hazel. Tate." Reaching out, Detective Bourgeois shook Tate's hand before touching Hazel on the arm.

"Detective," Hazel said, her limbs tingling. "Please come inside."

They settled into the living room, the air thick with anticipation. Detective Bourgeois cleared his throat before speaking, his eyes betraying the exhaustion of working tirelessly on the case.

"First off, I want you both to know that we are doing everything in our power to find Bella," he said, his voice steady yet tinged with urgency. "We've been working around the clock, following every lead we can."

"Any new developments?" Tate asked, leaning forward on the sofa with his elbows on his knees.

Rubbing his temples, Detective Bourgeois shook his head. "Unfortunately, not much has changed since our last update. We've questioned her family's friends and acquaintances, known sex offenders in the area. We've also combed through online activity, but so far, nothing substantial has come up."

Hazel's stomach churned at the thought of Bella out there, alone and frightened. She knew all too well how dangerous the world could be, especially when the paranormal was involved. Her fears threatened to consume her, but she forced herself to remain composed for Bella's sake.

"Thank you for your continued efforts, Detective." Bile burning in her throat, Hazel's voice wavered. "We know you're doing everything you can."

"Of course." The detective's eyes met hers, the seriousness of the matter etched into every line. "I won't rest until we find her and bring her home safe and sound."

Hazel's gaze drifted toward the window, the dim light casting eerie shadows across the room. The branches of a nearby tree swayed gently in the wind, their twisted limbs reaching out as if trying to grasp something just beyond their reach. The unsettling scene outside mirrored the growing turmoil inside her.

"Detective," Hazel began, her words hesitant as they tumbled through her mind. "I think I know why Bella was taken, and if I'm right, the suspect list would change completely."

Detective Bourgeois raised an eyebrow, his expression betraying a hint of curiosity. "What do you mean?"

"Dark magic." Doubt warring with the need to speak the truth in her mind, Hazel's fingers fumbled with the hem of her shirt. "I've been working with a witch in the area, looking into some old forms of necromancy that could potentially be involved."

"Old forms of…necromancy?" Detective Bourgeois repeated, clearly taken aback by the suggestion. "You mean, raising the dead?"

"Using Bella's powers to control the dead." Hazel shifted on the sofa, not knowing how to explain what she wanted so desperately to get across. "There are several cases in the past where dark practitioners have used these ancient arts to manipulate others, often for malicious purposes…even in New Orleans. Although I don't understand Bella's powers, she has them, and the person who has her may be using those powers to bend the spirits to their will."

"Interesting." Detective Bourgeois rubbed his chin, studying Hazel's face. "I must admit, I'm not exactly well-versed in the world of the supernatural. But if what you're saying is true, it could be worth expanding our suspect pool to include individuals who are at least said to practice dark magic. Although I'm not sure how difficult that will be. Do you have any idea what they're trying to accomplish?"

Hazel shook her head, although relief washed over her seeing the detective taking the idea seriously, not that she had doubted him. "That's what I'm trying to find out. At this point, I think he's trying to open the portal to the other side, allowing spirits to freely come back to the realm of the living."

Alarm showed in the detective's eyes as he blew out a breath. "I'm not sure what that means, but I'll see what I can dig up on the suspect side of things. In the meantime, if you find any information that might help us identify potential suspects, please let me know."

Although they still didn't have the suspect's identity, or the location where Bella was being kept, Hazel couldn't help but feel a renewed sense of determination pulsing through her veins. The thought of Bella in the clutches of someone wielding dark magic was horrifying, but at least they now had a new direction in their search, and the police force on their side.

Hazel's gaze swept over the cluttered dining room table, where Detective Bourgeois had spread out a map of South Louisiana with various locations marked in red.

Standing beside her, Tate's eyes narrowed as he studied the areas that had already been searched. "Can you give us an idea of where you've searched so far?"

"Of course."

For the next twenty minutes, the detective went over the map, explaining the searches that had been completed and those that were ongoing. Afterwards, they sat down at the table, drinking cups of coffee as he told them about police interviews they'd conducted.

The oxygen in the room seemed to thin as Detective Bourgeois continued recounting the details of their investigation, dread bringing a sour taste to the back of her mouth. The sense of urgency in her chest tightened like a vice, and she clenched her fists at her sides. Although Bella wasn't her family, she'd started to see her as something akin to a little sister.

"Every minute that passes makes me more worried for her," she confessed, her voice strained.

"Indeed." Detective Bourgeois nodded, a solemn expression on his face. "The longer she remains missing, the greater the risk becomes."

Wrapping his arm around Hazel's shoulder, Tate pulled her close, offering silent support. "We'll do everything we can to help you. Just let us know where we should start looking."

"Thank you." Detective Bourgeois stood, the gratitude on his face evident as he shook their hands. "I appreciate y'all's assistance, especially considering your unique expertise in these matters, Hazel."

The sky unleashed its fury, rain pounding in sheets against the windows as Hazel and Tate stood in thoughtful silence over the map Detective Bourgeois had left on their table. Candy had already vanished to conserve her energy, leaving it to them to discuss their plans. The air was thick with tension, Hazel's mind racing to process the information the detective had shared with them.

"Okay." Rubbing her temples, she closed her eyes, trying to process her thoughts one by one. "We need to figure out our next move. We can't just sit here while Bella's still missing."

Tate nodded, his expression serious. "Jeremiah mentioned a few places they searched, but there were some areas that caught my attention—specifically, the swampy area to the north of the interstate. It wasn't part of their initial search, but it's not a bad place to look."

Although the last place Hazel wanted to venture again was the swamp, she considered his idea. "You're right. It's worth checking out. If dark magic is involved, it wouldn't be surprising if whoever took Bella chose an isolated place like that. I really don't want to go back there, but we have to do something."

"I was afraid of that." Tate ran his hand through his hair, using the other to trace a line down Pearl River on the map.

With a sigh, Hazel lowered herself into a chair, overwhelmed by the entire situation. "I know, but we don't have much choice. She's just a little girl. We can't leave her alone there."

Tate placed a reassuring hand on Hazel's arm, offering her a small smile. "Don't worry. We'll find her, and we'll make sure whoever took her pays for what they've done."

"Thank you, baby," she said softly, gratitude filling her eyes. "I don't know what I would do without you."

As she looked up at her husband, memories of her past encounters with the dangerous parts of what she did resurfaced, and she worried about the toll it could take on them both. "Are you sure you're up for this?"

Reaching out, he squeezed her hand, his touch comforting. "I'll do anything to keep you safe, and I know we'll both do anything to bring that little girl back safe too."

Leaning over to kiss her on the cheek, a boyish grin curved up the side of his lips. "You're going to owe me two scoops of ice cream after this though."

Despite the gravity of the situation, Hazel couldn't help but smile. They'd faced perilous situations before, and she knew they made a formidable team, but she also knew, aside from the plane crash that had taken the lives of so many, that the stakes had never been higher.

With the map tucked safely in Tate's backpack, Hazel looked around their home, mentally ticking off items they would need for their search through the swamp. After all the cases she'd stumbled into over the years, she'd never before gone in without some sort of plan, which was saying something. The baby growing inside her meant she couldn't do things like she always had.

"Alright, let's start making a list." He pulled out a notepad and pen from a kitchen drawer, opening it to an empty page. "We'll need flashlights, extra batteries, rope, food, water, the first aid kid, and bug spray. Our rain boots are already in my trunk but I'll have to get some waders...although I would prefer to not bring you in any water deep enough to need them. They will help with snakes though."

Just the thought of it made Hazel cringe, but she pushed the fear away. No matter how afraid she was, it was nothing compared to how Bella must have been feeling at that moment. "And Tate...don't forget your gun. We don't know what we might encounter out there."

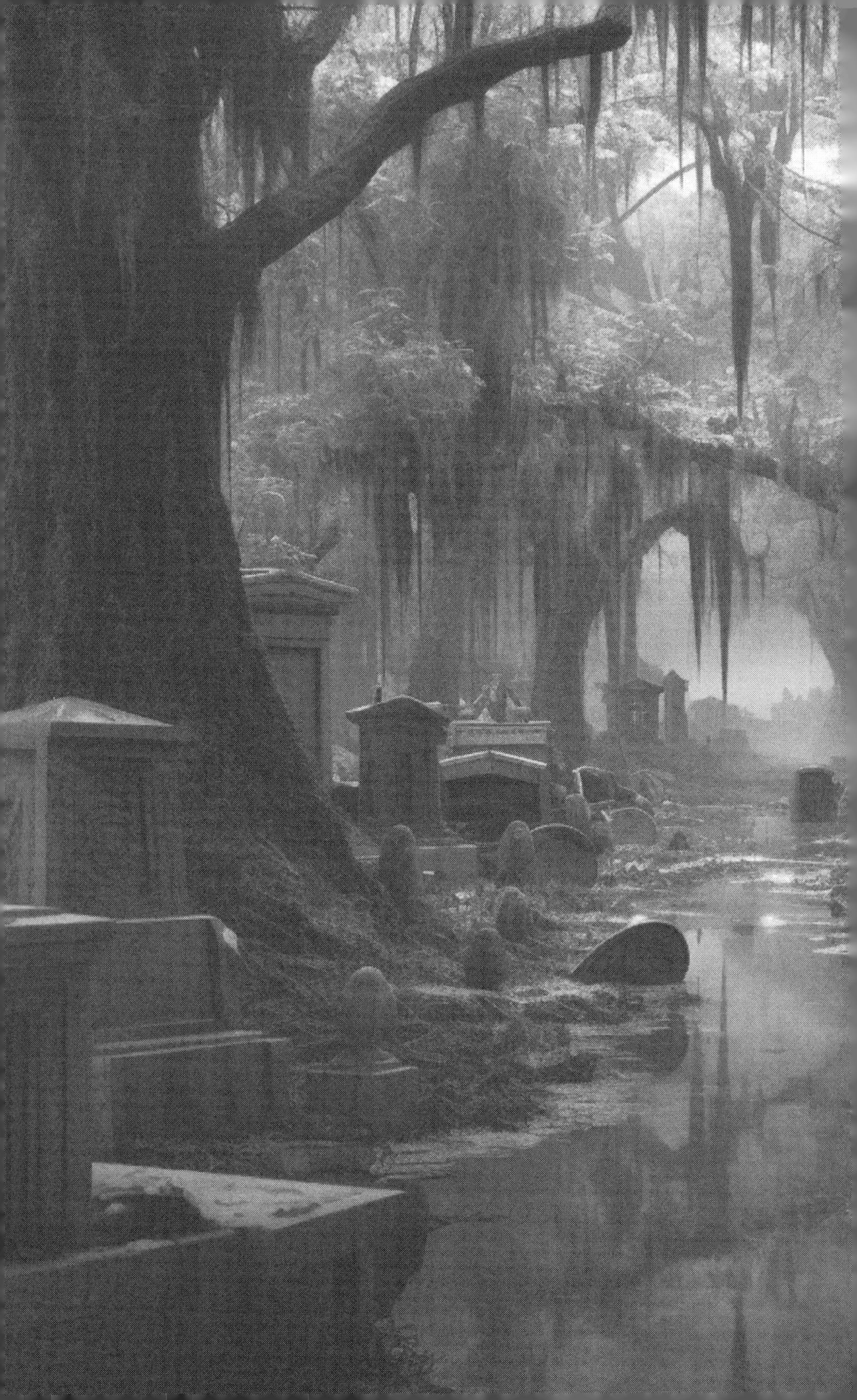

Chapter Fourteen
Returning to the Void

Hazel laid in bed, her eyes heavy with exhaustion, her mind yearning for the comfort of unconsciousness, if only to escape the overwhelming reality of her life for a few precious hours. The day had been long and draining, both physically and emotionally. The soft hum of the fan filled the room, providing a gentle lullaby that seemed to beckon her towards slumber. Trying to relax, her eyelids fluttered closed, and she could feel the first tendrils of darkness wrapping around her mind as she drifted into a deep slumber.

The world beyond her closed eyes seemed to recede further and further away, until Hazel was left alone in the abyss of her subconscious. The darkness enveloped her completely, leaving her vulnerable to the terrors that lurked within her own mind. It was within this inky void that her nightmares would come to life, taunting her with their twisted visions and haunting whispers.

As she sank deeper into the depths of her dreams, Hazel's thoughts began to fragment and scatter like leaves in the wind. Images from her past and present swirled around her, intertwining with the fears and uncertainties that plagued her waking hours. Her breathing slowed, and her heart rate steadied as she plunged headlong into the terrifying realm of her own subconscious mind, unaware of the chilling events that were about to transpire.

As the nightmares took hold, Hazel found herself standing in a twisted, desolate landscape. The ground beneath her feet was cracked and uneven, and the sky above seemed to be a swirling mass of dark clouds and malevolent shadows. Eerie whispers filled the air, their source impossible to discern as they echoed all around her.

"Help... please..."

"Leave... while you still can..."

A chill permeated to Hazel's bones as she took a tentative step forward, her legs shaky beneath her. "Who's there? Show yourself!"

As if in response to her defiance, shadowy figures began to emerge from the darkness, their forms spiraling and warping like smoke. They moved closer, surrounding her on all sides, their faces mere suggestions in the gloom—eyes that held pools of darkness and mouths that opened to release tortured screams.

"Get away from me!" Hazel cried out, trying to push through the encroaching shadows, but they clung to her like tar, pulling her further into their grasps. Panic swelled within her as she fought against the suffocating darkness.

"Please...we need you," one of the figures sobbed, its voice cracking with despair.

The desperation in its tone struck a chord deep within Hazel, and she paused for a moment, the misery around her sending ice through her veins. "Who are you?"

The shadows didn't respond, but instead, the scene around her shifted without warning. The darkness dissipated, leaving her standing in what appeared to be a vast void. It was a place she had encountered spirits in before—an otherworldly space where the thin veil between the living and the dead was all but nonexistent.

"Where am I?" Hazel whispered to herself, her eyes darting around the empty expanse. She knew that this place held answers, secrets she needed to uncover if she wanted to save those tormented souls who had reached out to her in her nightmares.

"Is anyone here?"

Despite the emptiness that stretched out before her, she couldn't shake the sensation that she was not alone.

"Remember...you're stronger than you think," a familiar voice echoed through the void, making her heart race with recognition.

"Who's there?" Eyes wide, she strained to see any signs of the speaker in the darkness. "Show yourself!"

A distant figure appeared before her, hovering just beyond reach, the form flickering like a candle flame, but before she could make out an identity, they disappeared into the blackness.

"Wait!" Hazel cried out, desperate for answers, but it was too late. The darkness swallowed her once more, dragging her back into the depths of her nightmares.

Suddenly, the void around Hazel changed again, revealing haunting images of Bella, Jake, and other missing spirits, their faces contorted in pain and despair. As their ghostly forms surrounded her, whispers filled the air, their voices an eerie chorus that felt like icy fingers crawling under her skin.

"Please...help us..." Bella's voice pleaded, her eyes wide with fear. "He's...too powerful..."

"Follow the star," Jake's faint voice urged, his expression grave. "Only you...can stop him..."

"Save us, Hazel," the others chimed in, their voices blending together in a desperate cacophony.

Dizziness wrapped around her head as she struggled to understand their cryptic messages. The urgency of their pleas only heightened her confusion and fear, leaving her grasping for any semblance of understanding. In the cold, dark air, their words hung like a heavy fog, clouding her thoughts and making it difficult to breathe.

"Wait!" She wanted to ask them more, but just as quickly as they'd appeared, the spirits vanished, leaving her alone in the void once more. Her hands clenched into fists at her sides, frustration and helplessness coursing through her veins.

While she wrestled with her thoughts, the void grew colder and darker, its oppressive weight threatening to crush her. However, a tiny spark of determination flickered within her, refusing to be extinguished despite the suffocating darkness. She couldn't ignore the suffering of those lost souls who reached out to her no matter how terrifying or uncertain the path ahead seemed.

While she closed her eyes, trying to cleanse herself from the fear that threatened to consume her, the shadows closed in, dragging her back into the nightmares that awaited her. With every passing moment, the line between reality and the supernatural realm blurred further, leaving Hazel to wonder if she would ever wake up.

Her breathing grew shallow as her surroundings altered once more, the darkness of the void giving way to another terrifying scene. This time, she found herself standing in an abandoned cemetery, the graves and crypts coated with grime and covered in vines that seemed to pulse like a dying heartbeat.

"Please...help us..." Bella's voice echoed through the eerie silence, a haunting plea that numbed Hazel's limbs, making it impossible to move.

"Where are you? What do I need to do?" Desperation twisted Hazel's chest, her voice quivering, but just as before, there was no answer, only the chilling whispers of the wind and the sinister shadows that danced around her.

The emotional toll of Hazel's nightmares weighed heavily on her heart, increasing her trepidation with each passing moment. In spite of her promise to save the missing spirits, she couldn't shake the feeling that she was running out of time, was in over her head, and that every second they spent in this horrific limbo brought them closer to a fate worse than death.

"Please," Hazel whispered, tears streaming down her face. "I'm trying my best. Just give me something to go on."

Hazel jolted awake before receiving her answer, her heart pounding, sweat coating her forehead. As she glanced around the dimly lit room, disoriented by the abrupt transition from the nightmare realm to her bedroom, Tate's sleeping form next to her sent relief washing over her.

The lingering shadows of her nightmares were pushed aside as she sat up in bed, watching his chest rise and fall, his dreams so much sweeter than her own. Taking a deep breath and pressing her hand against his chest, she tried to calm her racing heart. A sense of peace washed over her as the warmth of his body seeped into her fingertips, his strong heartbeat telling her they were very much alive, and as long as they were, she had the strength to help the others.

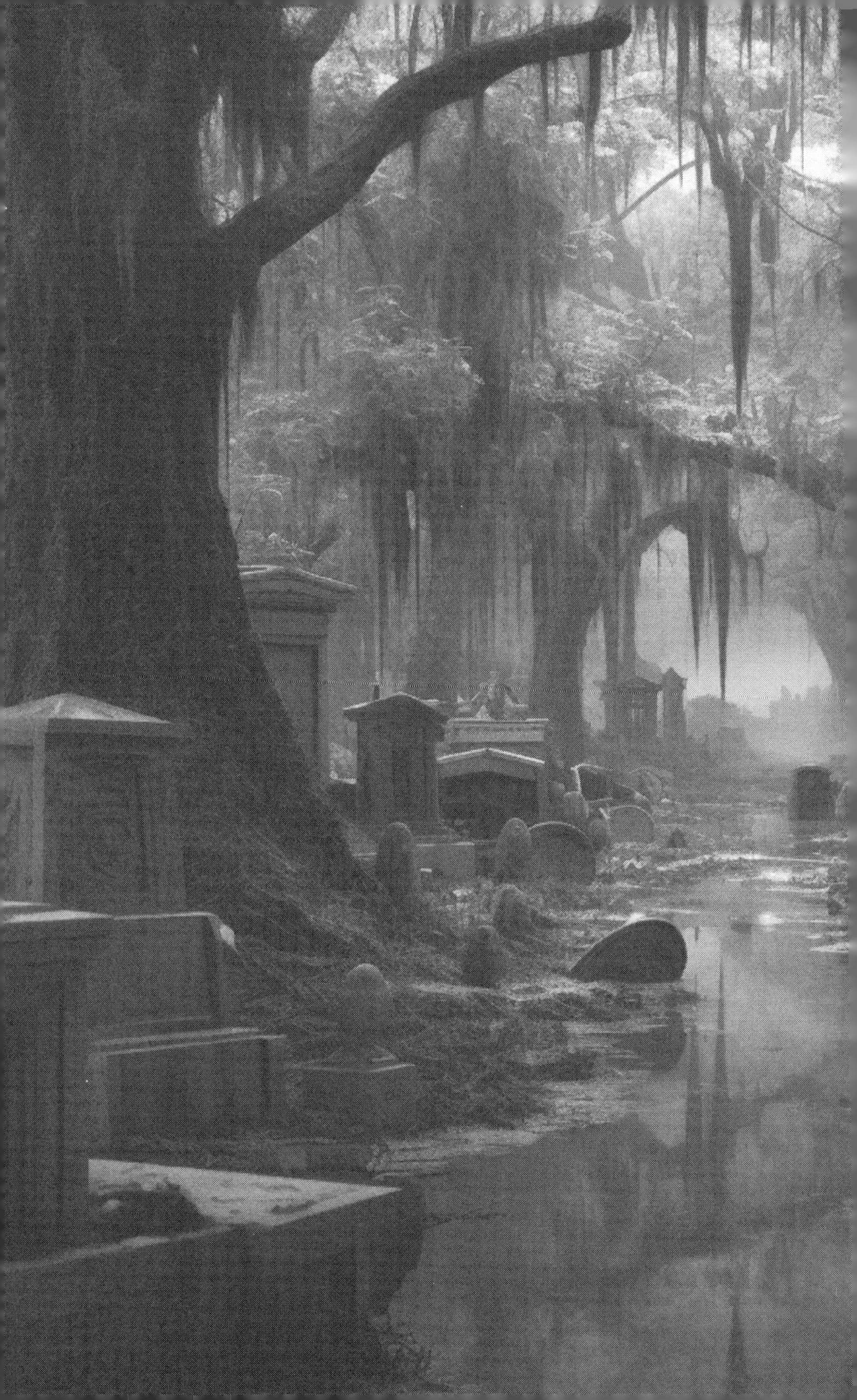

Chapter Fifteen
Venturing Into the Murky Water

The morning sun filtered through the blinds, casting a warm glow over the room as Hazel and Tate hastily gathered their supplies for the impending journey into the swamp. The air was thick with urgency, the weight of Hazel's task bearing down upon her.

"Make sure you grab the extra batteries for the flashlight," Hazel called out as she shoved food and water into a bag. "And don't forget the first aid kit."

"Got it," Tate replied, his brow furrowed in concentration as he double-checked their inventory.

Candy floated around the house as they worked, the nervous energy pulsing off her in waves. "Did Tate tell the detective where y'all are going—just in case y'all need backup?"

Blowing out a breath as morning sickness crept back up her esophagus, Hazel nodded. "Detective Bourgeois knows we're going north. They'll keep their distance until Tate calls them on the two-way radio."

Seeming to be satisfied, Candy vanished, needing to conserve her energy for the potential fight ahead.

As Hazel stuffed a few more items into her backpack, she caught a glimpse of herself in the hallway mirror. Dark circles rimmed her eyes, her face appearing gaunt from the stress, morning sickness, and lack of sleep. She turned away from the mirror quickly, her hands trembling as she zipped up her bag.

"Are you okay?" Moving to her side, Tate placed a hand on the small of her back.

She leaned into his strong body, closing her eyes and willing the nausea to pass. No matter what she was going through, he was always her rock. "Yeah. I'm just...nervous."

"We'll find them, love," he said, leaning forward to kiss her forehead. "We're in this together."

Looking into his eyes, she managed a small smile. As much as she appreciated Tate's comforting words, and his unwavering support, an unsettling sense of dread filled her chest, threatening to suffocate her. She couldn't shake the feeling that they were walking into a situation that could very well cost them their lives and that was a fate she couldn't accept. Still, she couldn't ignore her obligations either.

"Okay." With a nod, she pulled away, her grip tightening on the straps of her backpack. "Let's do this."

The drive north on the interstate was accompanied by an uneasy silence. Hazel's fingers tapped restlessly against the steering wheel as they passed an endless parade of billboards and fast-food joints. A sense that something was amiss plagued her, gnawing at her gut like an insistent itch she couldn't quite reach.

As they continued driving toward the outskirts of the city, the landscape gradually changed from urban to rural. Skyscrapers and traffic gave way to trees and wetlands. The sun continued to move across the sky, backlighting the ominous black clouds that threatened a thunderstorm.

"Are you sure you don't want me to drive?" Tate asked, concern etched on his face as he watched Hazel's knuckles turn white from gripping the steering wheel.

"I'm okay." Even as she loosened her grip, her voice betrayed the tension simmering beneath her skin. "With all the chaos, I just needed to feel in control of something."

"Hey," Tate said, rubbing her shoulder. "Remember, we're in this together. Whatever happens, we'll face it side by side."

Glancing in the rearview mirror, she nodded, although the empty backseat only filled her with more dread. Instead of sitting in the backseat making faces at her, Candy was still conserving her energy, but as long as Candy wasn't within the protected walls of their house, Hazel knew she wouldn't be able to stop worrying about her vanishing. If she lost her best friend, she didn't know what she would do. "I know. I just can't shake this feeling...like we're being watched, and like something really bad is going to happen."

"Everything is going to be okay, love." Tate's hand slid onto her thigh, giving it a reassuring squeeze. "You're stronger than you think, Hazel, and the police are standing by to move in the moment we find Bella."

"There," Tate said, pointing out the window. "There's the turnoff for where we're headed."

Blowing out a cleansing breath, she nodded and eased the car onto the exit ramp.

As they parked on the side of the road near the most navigable part of the swamps north of the Pearl River, the headlights cast eerie shadows on the gnarled trees and murky water. The sun slid behind the dark clouds, leaving the place deeply shadowed. She turned off the engine, and suddenly the only sounds were the chorus of cicadas and the distant croaking of frogs. The humidity was oppressive, clinging to her skin like a damp blanket.

"Ugh, I hate this place," she muttered as she climbed out of the car, her voice betraying her unease. Unable to help herself, her mind automatically turned to her first time venturing into the swamps, when the serial killer, Raymond Waters, had knocked her unconscious and thrown her into the trunk of his car. She had come full circle since then, this time choosing to wade into the swamps willingly, but it was no less dangerous.

Taking in a deep breath, the scent of decaying plants and stagnant water made her stomach churn. It was a far cry from the crisp fall air that had greeted them back at their home in the suburbs south of the city.

"Hey," Tate said, placing a reassuring hand on her shoulder. "We're going to find Bella, Jake, and the missing spirits. No matter what. And then we'll take really long showers and sleep in our own bed."

Tucking the amulet Celeste had given her for protection into her shirt, Hazel smiled. "I look forward to that."

Searching her face for a few heartbeats longer, Tate opened the trunk of the car. "Alright, let's make sure we have everything." His practical nature taking over, he checked their supplies, ensuring they were prepared for any challenges that awaited them.

The air was heavy with humidity, the buzzing of insects filling Hazel's ears like a haunting chorus. Setting their shoes into the trunk, both Hazel and Tate pulled on waders to protect their lower body from standing water and snakes. The sense of foreboding in Hazel's chest intensified, but she had come too far to turn back.

"Ready?" she asked, her heart racing with a mix of anticipation and dread.

Scanning the tree line, Tate nodded, holstering his service pistol on his waist and closing the trunk of the car. "Remember, stay close to me. There are a lot of dangers out here."

Hazel's breath hitched as she stepped into the trees, feeling the muddy ground squelch beneath her boots. Reappearing by her side, Candy hovered a few feet above the ground, her ethereal form shimmering in the dappled sunlight that briefly broke through the clouds and filtered through the thick canopy of trees above.

"Do you feel anything, doll? I can't sense him here. I can't sense any of them."

Closing her eyes, Hazel focused on her sixth sense, but aside from an ever growing feeling of unease, she didn't sense any spirits nearby—none aside from the spirit beside her. "I don't sense any spirits, but something here feels...wrong...like we shouldn't be here."

Candy huffed, lowering herself to the ground until she was walking beside them. "We're rarely where we're supposed to be when you start chasing ghosts."

Walking on her other side, Tate repeated Candy's sentiment as he pulled out the two-way radio, letting the detective know they had made it to the location.

"Careful," Tate murmured, his hand brushing against hers as they picked their way through the dense vegetation. "We don't know what's lurking in here. Just watch where you step."

Even with the waders on, the last thing Hazel wanted to step on was an alligator or a water moccasin. "Candy, can you go ahead and up high, see if you can find any abandoned structures, anything man-made. If he is out here, I doubt he's hanging out in the trees."

With a nod, Candy vanished, leaving Hazel and Tate alone once again.

As they ventured deeper into the swamp, the sounds of wildlife grew increasingly distant, replaced by an unnerving silence that made her stomach tense. Each breath she took felt as if it were filled with an oppressive weight. She clutched Tate's hand tighter, seeking reassurance from his familiar warmth. Just as she was starting to worry about her friend, Candy reappeared beside her.

"Seems like the necromancer doesn't want us to find him," Candy murmured, her spectral form glowing faintly in the gloom. "But there is a clearing not far north. I sensed other floaters, but I didn't see any."

Although she still couldn't sense other spirits nearby, Hazel's eyes scanned the eerie surroundings for any signs of movement.

"Can you see anything, love?" Tate asked as he handed her a bottle of water.

Her body already dehydrated and exhausted, she took the bottle without question, taking a deep drink. When she was finished, she shook her head, wrapping her arms around her chest. "Something is dampening my abilities but Candy found a clearing to the north. Maybe we can rest there and reassess our direction."

"You know..." Tate hesitated for a moment, pulling out his compass to check their direction. "You mentioned Jake telling you to follow the star—or find the star–I'm not sure of the wording you used. Do you think he could have been talking about the north star? Maybe he was giving you directions the best way he knew how."

Even though Hazel hadn't yet deciphered Jake's cryptic message, she considered Tate's suggestion. "Everytime I see Bella in the void, there's a star inside a circle on her hand. I saw the same symbol inside a book in the spirit realm."

"Uh, doll." Icy fingers grabbed Hazel's wrist, interrupting her explanation. She stopped walking, her eyes drawn to the direction Candy was pointing. "Does the symbol look like that one?"

Straight ahead of them, the same image she'd seen on Bella's wrist was carved into the trunk of a cypress tree. She walked ahead, tracing the shape with her fingers.

"This is it." The shape seemed to pulse with energy beneath her fingers, sending an electric charge through her body. "This is the symbol I was talking about. I believe it's been used by witches over time, but from what I've uncovered online, this same symbol has been used by necromancers as well."

Tate moved in beside her, marking their location on his phone. "This can't be a coincidence."

As Hazel continued to examine the shape, Candy's voice called out to her further up their path. "There's another one up here!"

Abandoning the first tree, Hazel chased the sound of Candy's voice, Tate on her heels. When they arrived at the second tree, she found the same shape carved into the trunk. "Maybe these are the stars we are supposed to be following."

Even as she said it, another thought tumbled into her mind, one she didn't want to acknowledge. Although she wanted to think the symbols were a good sign—like breadcrumbs left for her to find her way—there was also a chance the symbols were drawn by the necromancer as part of a spell or ritual. If that was the case, then continuing on further could only put them in more danger. Glancing at her husband beside her, indecision squeezed Hazel's chest. The last thing she wanted to do was put him or the child in her stomach in danger. Still, she knew what was at stake, so she didn't give the warning in her mind any more attention by speaking it out loud. No matter the risks, they had to keep moving forward.

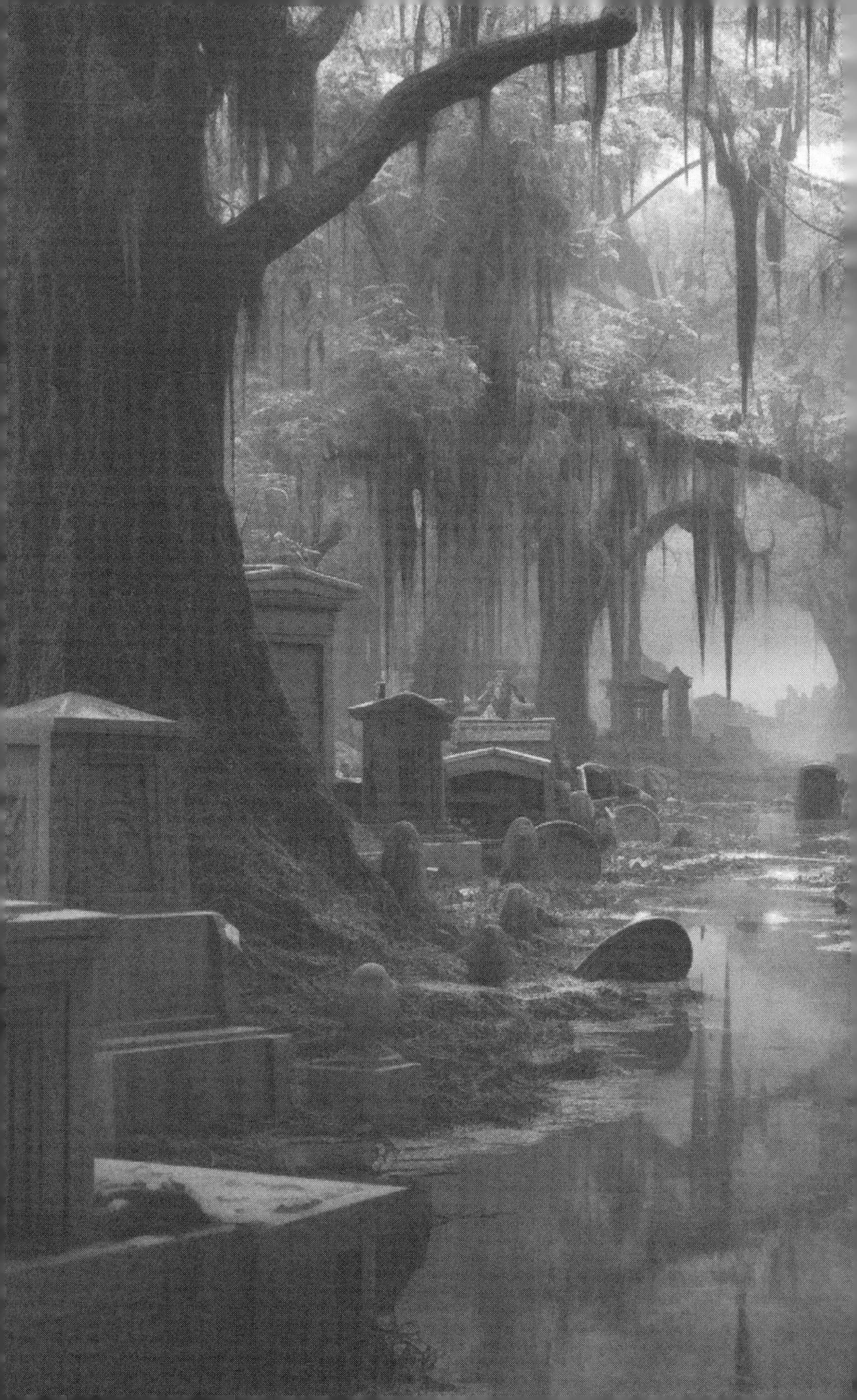

Chapter Sixteen

Beacon of Hope in the Darkness

The thick tendrils of mist curled around Hazel's legs as she pushed through the swamp. They walked north, guided by Tate's compass as well as the symbols etched into the trees. She refused to allow the muddy ground to slow her down, even though it sucked at her boots with each step like quicksand. Tate was beside her, his eyes scanning their surroundings, while Candy floated above them, casting a glistening light on the dark foliage from her translucent form.

"Ugh," Hazel grumbled, swatting away a mosquito. "I hate swamps."

"Me too," Tate said, wincing as he stepped over a twisted root. "But if this is where we have to go to save Jake, Bella, and everyone else, then so be it."

Floating by their side, Candy giggled at their misery, since her spectral form prevented her from having to slosh through muck or being eaten alive by bird-sized mosquitoes.

Without warning, the silence was shattered by rustling in the underbrush. Before anyone could react, spirits emerged from the shadows, their twisted faces contorted with pain, their eyes empty. As though under a spell, they surrounded Hazel, Tate, and Candy, leaving no escape route.

Before Hazel could react, Candy threw out her arms, forcing the spirits back. The amulet around Hazel's neck warmed, creating a shimmering barrier around them.

"What the—" Wrapping his arm around her waist, Tate pulled Hazel closer to him, his body language on high alert although he couldn't see the threat. Candy remained beside them, her form flickering before flaring back strongly.

"There are spirits," Hazel whispered under her breath, needing to explain to Tate what she was seeing. "They have us surrounded, but something is wrong with them."

With ice freezing her veins and making it difficult to move, Hazel wrapped her hand around Tate's and forced one foot to fall in front of the other. "We need to keep moving. They're staying back for now, but they're watching us."

Tate nodded, but Hazel could tell by the tension in his body that even he felt their cold, malevolent presence just inches from them.

"Thank you, Candy," Hazel breathed, her heart racing as she watched one of the spirits crash against the barrier, their clawed hands reaching out to grasp at her and Tate. "We'd be lost without you."

"You're welcome, doll, but we need to keep moving. I don't know if that amulet will hold them off forever."

They continued to navigate the treacherous terrain, the sky growing darker with every step. Hours seemed to stretch into days as they delved deeper into the heart of the swamp, the oppressive atmosphere only growing more palpable with each passing moment.

"Hey." Stopping unexpectedly, Tate pointed ahead. "Do you see that?"

Hazel squinted in the direction he indicated, and after a moment, she saw it too–a faint glimmer of light in the distance, shining like a beacon of hope amidst the darkness.

"Could that be...?" As she continued to peer into the trees ahead, mist swirling up from the ground like serpents, Hazel's voice trailed off.

"There's only one way to find out," Tate replied, speaking low into the radio to notify the police of where they were before marking the location on his GPS. "Should we check it out?"

Although Hazel was terrified to move forward, she knew they had no choice. The spirits hovering behind them seemed to be herding them toward the light. Turning back and risking being overwhelmed by them would be the only alternative. As Tate's reassuring hand held hers, she squared her shoulders and kept walking.

As they moved closer to the light, Hazel's thoughts raced, a mixture of dread and fierce determination powering her movements. The swamp appeared to close in around them, but the spirits maintained their distance with the barrier still providing protection. The air was heavy with humidity, and Hazel could feel beads of sweat trickling down her spine, despite the cool breeze that occasionally whispered through the trees.

"Look," Tate murmured, pointing toward the small clearing in the swamp, the place where the sickly sour smell of despair seemed to emanate. "There it is."

The eerie atmosphere intensified as they moved toward the light. The twisted branches of ancient trees loomed overhead like the arms of a monster, casting grotesque shadows that danced across the ghostly mist. The sounds of unseen creatures slithered and whispered around them, their origins impossible to pinpoint, which only disturbed Hazel more.

Approaching the place where plant life didn't dare grow, Hazel's heart became sluggish as she strained her ears, listening to the haunting echoes that drifted through the fog. Every now and then, she caught the faintest hint of a mournful wail or a sobbing whisper, tantalizingly close yet somehow out of reach. It was as if the very air around them was alive with the voices of the dead, beckoning them further into the depths of the swamp.

When they entered the clearing, a crypt, previously hidden from view, loomed before them, partially submerged in the muck, its dark stone walls slick with moss and algae. On the very top of the stone structure was a sculpture of a star, a decaying wreath of flowers hanging from it in the shape of a circle. It was a chilling sight in the midst of the swamp, and though she had steeled herself against fear, an involuntary shudder ran through her.

"Are you sure you're ready for this?" Tate asked, his voice low and tense, his eyes searching hers for any signs of doubt.

"As ready as I'm gonna be." Although Hazel's voice was steady, her thoughts were anything but calm. She couldn't help but worry about what lay ahead, about the dangers they would surely face inside the crypt, but her determination to save Bella, Jake, and the missing spirits outweighed her fears. "But I'm definitely going to want that ice cream if I make it out of this alive—two scoops."

"Two scoops it is." Chuckling, Tate leaned over and kissed her, lingering on her lips long enough to defrost some of her insides. When he pulled away, Tate squeezed her hand, turning her to face the entrance to the crypt. "Ready?"

Taking a deep breath and blowing it out slowly, Hazel nodded, Candy speaking in unison with her, "Ready."

The darkness inside the massive crypt was almost suffocating, broken only by the faint flicker of torchlight that danced across the damp walls. Unlike most crypts, which were one large room meant to hold the remains of a family, the space that surrounded them was sprawling, with a main corridor and several rooms on either side. The floor had crumbled away, leaving the ground at their feet flooded with swamp water, making it dangerous to walk through. Hazel strained her ears for any sounds beyond their own footsteps, but the crypt was eerily silent.

Pulling out his gun and flicking on his flashlight, Tate took the lead. "Stay close to me," he whispered, his breath warm against her ear. "And take this."

Hazel nodded, hesitating for only a moment before taking the machete from him and holding it tight in her hand as they continued forward. She could feel Candy's spectral presence beside them, a comforting reminder that they were not alone in their quest. There was still a lingering fear in Hazel's mind that the necromancer would take

Candy away from her, but her best friend had proven time and time again how powerful she was—she had saved Hazel more than once–so it was time that Hazel started having faith in her power to do so.

Grabbing the back of Tate's shirt, Hazel pulled him to a stop, her instincts screaming at her and warning her of unseen dangers lurking in the shadows. "Something doesn't feel right."

When Tate turned around, he slid his hand up to cup her cheek, the touch reassuring. "Trust your instincts, love. We'll face whatever comes our way, together. The police aren't far away if we need them."

Closing her eyes to savor Tate's touch a moment longer, Hazel nodded. "My instincts are telling me that I need to walk in first. You may have the gun, but the dangers ahead will be supernatural. I'm hoping this amulet helps us against that."

Tate didn't respond right away, the war in his mind clear in his eyes. Hazel knew he wanted to face the danger first—that was the police officer and protective husband in him–but Hazel also knew she was right. Out of the three of them, she needed to go forward.

With one more kiss to her lips, Tate nodded and moved aside, handing the flashlight to her. "You can go ahead but please wait for me. Please don't run ahead and put yourself in danger."

The flashlight created eerie shadows on the walls as they delved deeper into the crypt. Hazel's heart pounded in her ears, and although she didn't see anyone else around them, she couldn't shake the feeling that they were being watched. The air grew colder as they approached the entrance to the main chamber, and the sickening taste of dread crept up her throat.

The rotting wooden door creaked open, a sliver of light piercing the inky blackness within. Hazel peered into the yawning void, her breaths coming in short, ragged gasps. Stealing herself, she slipped inside, fingers twitching on the handle of the machete she held in her hand.

As she crept through the dusty corridors, the fetid stench of decay assaulted her nostrils. Strange scuttling sounds echoed from the shadows, raising the hairs on the back of her neck. She swallowed hard, willing her thundering heart to slow.

Up ahead, a pulsing purple light seeped from an archway, its illumination wholly unearthly. Hazel's stomach churned, but she forced herself onward. She had to find Bella.

When Hazel stepped into the cavernous chamber, her eyes fell upon a huddled form chained to the far wall. "Bella!" she cried just before the door slammed shut behind her.

A raspy chuckle slithered from the darkness. "Welcome. We've been waiting for you." A tall, skeletal figure draped in tattered black robes emerged into the purple glow. *The necromancer.* Although she could tell he was a man, she couldn't make out his features with the hood of his robe masking his face.

Hand tightening on her weapon, Hazel's lip curled. "Let her go."

The necromancer tilted his head, black eyes glinting. "Now why would I do that when her power will fuel my reign?"

Hazel's gut twisted at his vile words. She had to distract him, buy time to get to Bella. Fists pounded on the door as Tate tried to find his way into the room with her, but Hazel returned her eyes to the little girl cowering in the corner.

"Your reign? You're nothing but a spineless coward to pick on an innocent child."

As the necromancer's face contorted in rage, Hazel held her breath, poised to strike.

Without warning, his spindly hand shot out, crackling with dark energy. Hazel dove and rolled, the bolt sizzling past her ear. When she popped up, she slashed at his robes, the machete's blade flashing. He recoiled with an angry hiss.

"Foolish girl," he snarled. "You cannot stop what is to come."

A second later, he began chanting sinister words that seemed to suck the very air from the room. The temperature plummeted as shadows swirled and took shape, forming leering specters.

At the sight of the wraiths surrounding her, Hazel's heart sank to the floor, but she held her ground. She had to keep the necromancer focused on her and away from Bella, who appeared to be unconscious—at least until Tate or the police found their way inside the room.

With a feral cry, she launched herself at him again, her blade biting deep into his shoulder. Howling, he backhanded her, sending her crashing to the stone floor. Pain exploded in her shoulder and the metallic tang of blood covered her tongue. She tried to get up again, but she was dazed, fear nearly paralyzing her.

"Hazel!" Bella's panicked voice cut through the haze, jolting Hazel back into reality. Hazel's eyes flew open to see a wraith swooping toward the chained little girl, its skeletal hands outstretched.

Maternal fury erupted in Hazel's chest. She was on her feet in an instant, hurtling toward Bella. She collided with the wraith in midair, her amulet flaring hot against her chest. With an unearthly wail, the specter dissipated.

Panting, Hazel placed herself between Bella and the necromancer, the remaining wraiths hissing at her like rabid animals.

"Help is coming, Bella," she said, her eyes never leaving the threats in front of her. "It's going to be okay."

As the necromancer turned his back to her to reach for his dagger, an icy breeze stirred Hazel's hair. Candy slid into the room through the stone wall, her blue eyes filled with fire. Before Hazel knew what was happening, her best friend's spectral form slipped inside her body. Although they'd practiced Candy manipulating her dreams before, Candy had never tried to possess her—at least not with her knowledge.

"Help is coming, doll." The words came to Hazel through her subconsciousness. "Until then, he can fight both of us."

Hazel's palms tingled as invisible hands took hold of hers, power thrumming through her veins that far exceeded her own. When her eyes flew open, they glowed silver.

Faltering at the sight, uncertainty flickered across the necromancer's face. Taking advantage of his temporary confusion, Hazel lifted the machete, the weapon blazing with ethereal fire.

With a scream that wasn't totally her own, Hazel charged the wraiths. Her weapon cut through them like smoke. In moments, only ashes remained on the floor.

Chest heaving, she rounded on the necromancer, Candy's spirit within her making her fear all but disappear. With a wave of his hand, he hurled a bolt of dark energy at her, but her reflexes were quicker, her body leaping to the side just in time. The energy from his spell hit the wall with a force that created a large gash in the stone, fragments of it hitting the floor only feet from where Bella lay.

"You're fighting a losing battle," she said, her voice holding more confidence than she'd ever possessed.

Whatever the necromancer saw in her eyes made his own widen. He turned to reach for something on the table, but Hazel was upon him in an instant, taking the dagger from his hand and pressing it to his throat. Although he was much larger than her, Candy's power inside her gave her a strength beyond her own comprehension. The banging outside the door got louder, telling her Tate was close to breaking down the door.

As she held the necromancer there, with the dagger poised at his throat, she took in his appearance for the first time. What surprised her more than anything was that he was young—no older than thirty—with long black hair and skin pale enough that he almost looked dead. He looked at her with contempt, his dark eyes like depthless pits.

"Go ahead, end it." His body relaxed, no longer struggling in her grasp. "But you know it won't stop my plans. Others will rise to take my place."

Hazel pressed the blade harder, drawing a trickle of blood.

"I should kill you," she said, the words surprising even her. "But I won't become a murderer for your sake."

Keeping the dagger ready, she stepped back when a piece of the door gave way, Tate's screams breaking through the tense air.

Her enemy let out a mocking laugh. "You're weak, just like that little girl. I'll make sure she and your spawn suffer for your mercy."

Rage boiled up in Hazel and she started to lunge forward, but stopped herself. That was what he wanted—to goad her into killing, but she wouldn't give him the satisfaction.

As they stared at each other, both waiting for the other to make the first move, the heavy wooden door splintered, flying open. Tate stood in the doorway, his gun pointed at the necromancer's head. Several police officers flooded into the room around him, taking the necromancer to his knees.

Once the fiend was in handcuffs, Candy slid out of Hazel's body, moving to stand by her side. A heartbeat later, Tate darted across the room, her body sagging with exhaustion when his arms wrapped around her, the adrenaline in her blood draining away.

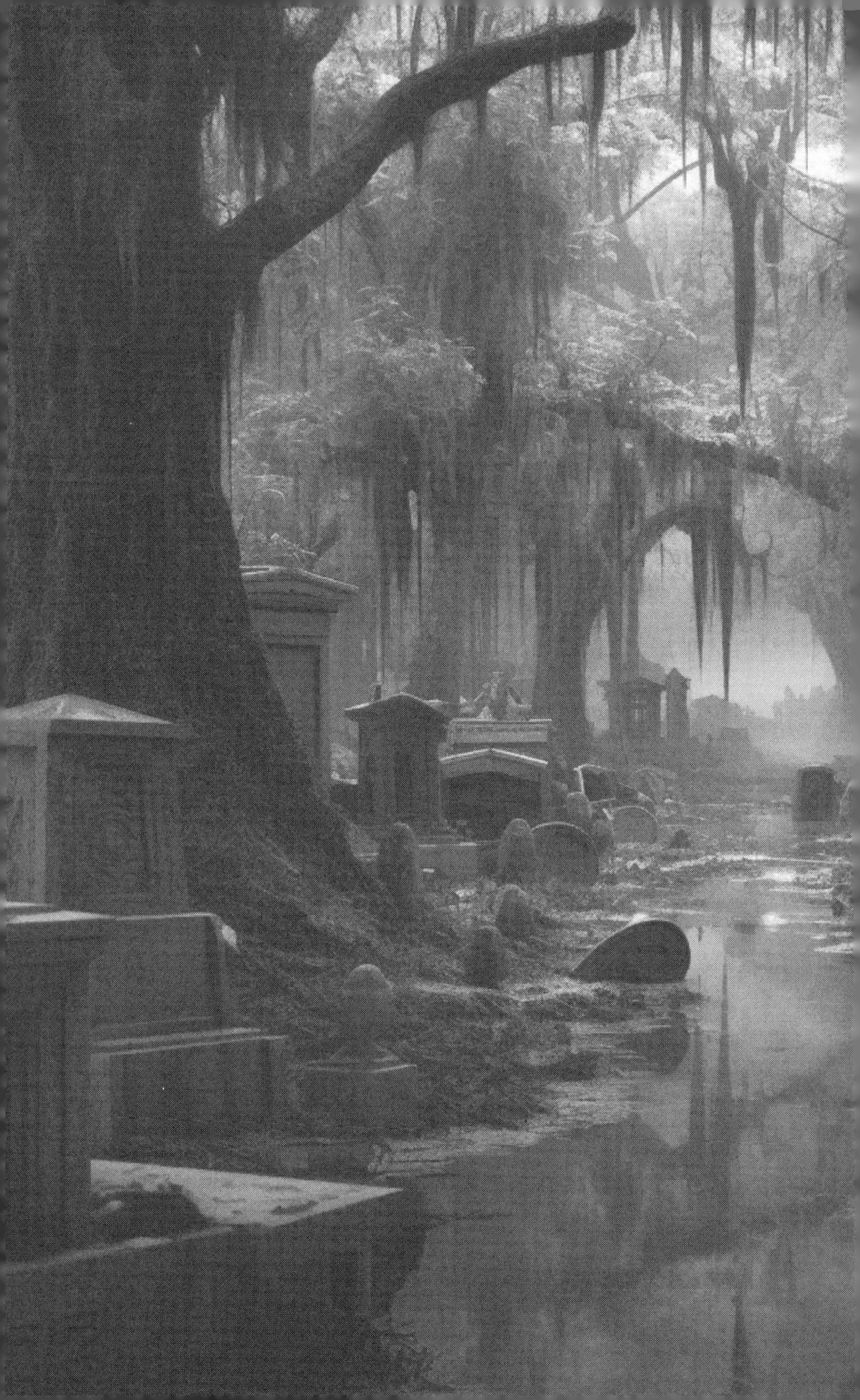

Chapter Seventeen
Crossing Into the Light

"Bella!" Hazel's energy surged as she and Tate rushed to Bella's unconscious body, her limbs zinging with energy. The little girl lay chained to the wall, her face deathly pale under the crypt's dim light. As they approached, the sound of hurried footsteps echoed behind them, relief washing over Hazel when the officers moved past them to attend to her.

"Easy, sweetheart," one officer whispered, his hands gentle as he worked on the restraints. Hazel watched him closely, her protective instincts still on high alert despite the presence of the law.

"Let's get her out of here," another officer said once Bella was free, lifting her small frame and carrying her out of the crypt.

Her exhaustion from the fight finally catching up with her, Hazel leaned against her husband. She could feel every bruise, every cut, every strained muscle in her battered body, but despite her own pain, all she could think about was Bella's well-being.

"Please let her be okay," Hazel whispered, her eyes following the policemen until they disappeared into the corridor with Bella.

Legs finally giving out from exhaustion, Hazel's knees buckled, nearly dropping her to the ground.

"Whoa there," Tate said, concern etching his handsome features as he scooped her up as though she weighed nothing, holding her close against his chest. "You're no good to anyone if you collapse."

Sighing, she rested her head against his chest, allowing him to carry her out of the crypt. The air in the swamp was thick with the scent of decay, but also carried a newfound sense of hope. She wrapped her arms around Tate's neck, feeling the steady rise and fall of his chest beneath her cheek.

"Fine, but only because I don't want to walk anymore," she grumbled, refusing to admit she needed help. In truth, she appreciated Tate's protectiveness, even when she fought against it.

As they made their way out of the crypt and into the clearing, the police were busy securing the necromancer in handcuffs. His once-menacing presence seemed pathetic and small as he thrashed and cursed at them, spitting dark threats of vengeance. The officers seemed completely unphased as they escorted him into the swamp and out of sight.

"See those medics over there?" Tate nodded toward the group of officers and EMTs who had Bella between them, the little girl still unconscious. "They're going to check you out, okay?"

"Ugh, fine." Although Hazel didn't want to take any of the attention off of Bella, she was pregnant, so she knew getting checked was best. "Fine, but you're going to owe me two scoops after this."

"Deal," Tate agreed, pressing a soft kiss to her temple before stepping back to give the medics room to work.

Hazel clenched her jaw as they inspected her bruises and scrapes, forcing herself to focus on anything but the uncomfortable prodding. While they worked, she glanced around, searching for any sign of the spirits that had been trapped by the necromancer's dark magic.

"Miss, you're good to go," the medic said, helping her off the stretcher. "Just make sure to take it easy for a few days."

Moving to her side, Tate lifted her into his arms and took a few steps out of the paramedic's way

As if sensing her thoughts, the shadows in the clearing began to shimmer and shift, revealing dozens of spirits emerging from their hiding places. Among them was Jake, his ethereal form flickering, his mouth stretching into a smile the moment he spotted Hazel.

"Jake!" Flying across the clearing, Candy's crimson hair was like a burst of flame as she tackled the man she loved, jumping on him like a spectral spider monkey. "You're okay!"

Hazel watched their reunion from her place in her husband's arms, happy tears bursting their way to the surface.

"Jake's back," she said, relaxing into Tate's warmth. "They all are."

While she watched Candy and Jake embrace, the newly freed spirits floated in Hazel's direction.

"Thank you," a female spirit murmured, her eyes brimming with tears as she looked at Hazel. "You've saved us all."

"Indeed," another spirit agreed, a man dressed in a gray military uniform. "We owe you a debt we can never repay."

One-by-one, the spirits continued to express their appreciation before fading away, crossing over to the other side. Each of them left behind an aura of serenity, as though they were finally able to rest after an eternity of torment. All except for Jake and Candy, who remained by Hazel and Tate's side.

"Family sticks together, right, doll?" The smile on Candy's stunning face couldn't have gotten any brighter than it was at that moment with Jake's arm wrapped around her waist.

Hazel nodded, reaching forward to touch Candy's hand. "You better not go into that light or I'm gonna go in after you."

Although he could only hear part of the conversation, Tate chuckled. "You better not go into the light anytime soon, my love."

Wrapping her arm around Tate's neck, Hazel tilted her face upward, pulling him into a kiss. "You better not either. All three of you are my family, and this baby will need all of us to protect it from this crazy world."

As they lingered in the clearing, watching as the spirits crossed over, the medics disappeared into the swamp with Bella, leaving Hazel's heart aching for the little girl. She knew she'd done everything she could to save her, but worry still gnawed at her insides.

"Will she be okay?" she asked, her voice barely audible.

Tate tightened his arm around her, offering what comfort he could. "She's strong, just like you. I have faith that she'll pull through."

Hazel closed her eyes, taking solace in Tate's words and allowing herself to be enveloped in his embrace. "Thank you, Tate, for everything."

Leaning down, Tate kissed her again, his eyes filled with love. "Anything for you. We're in this together, remember? Come on," he said, holding her tighter. "Let's go home."

She nodded, her tired eyes meeting Jake and Candy's. "Home sounds perfect."

The scent of decaying foliage and stagnant water filled Hazel's nose, the sounds of night creatures echoing around them as they navigated the swamp. Jake and Candy floated alongside them, an ethereal presence that glowed softly in the moonlight.

"Did you ever think we'd be here?" Hazel asked, her gaze lifting to meet Tate's. "I mean, really... Did you ever imagine we'd be fighting necromancers to save spirits and a little girl?"

Tate chuckled, shaking his head. "Not in my wildest dreams, but I wouldn't change it for anything. We've made a difference, Hazel. You made a difference. I know it's been tough, but we did it together."

When they stepped out of the tree line, the first light of dawn painted the sky a brilliant array of pinks and oranges. The trees rustled in the wind, and the sound of birds chirping reminding Hazel of the life that lived within the swamp. It was a promise of a new day, a reminder that life continued to march forward, no matter how dark the night had been. Hazel took a deep breath and let the weight of the night lifted from her shoulders.

"Look at that," she whispered, awestruck by the sunrise's beauty. "It's like the world is telling us that we can start anew."

"Then let's do just that." Tate kissed her again, setting her down on the ground beside the car and helping remove her waders. "We can start by cleaning all this mud off of us."

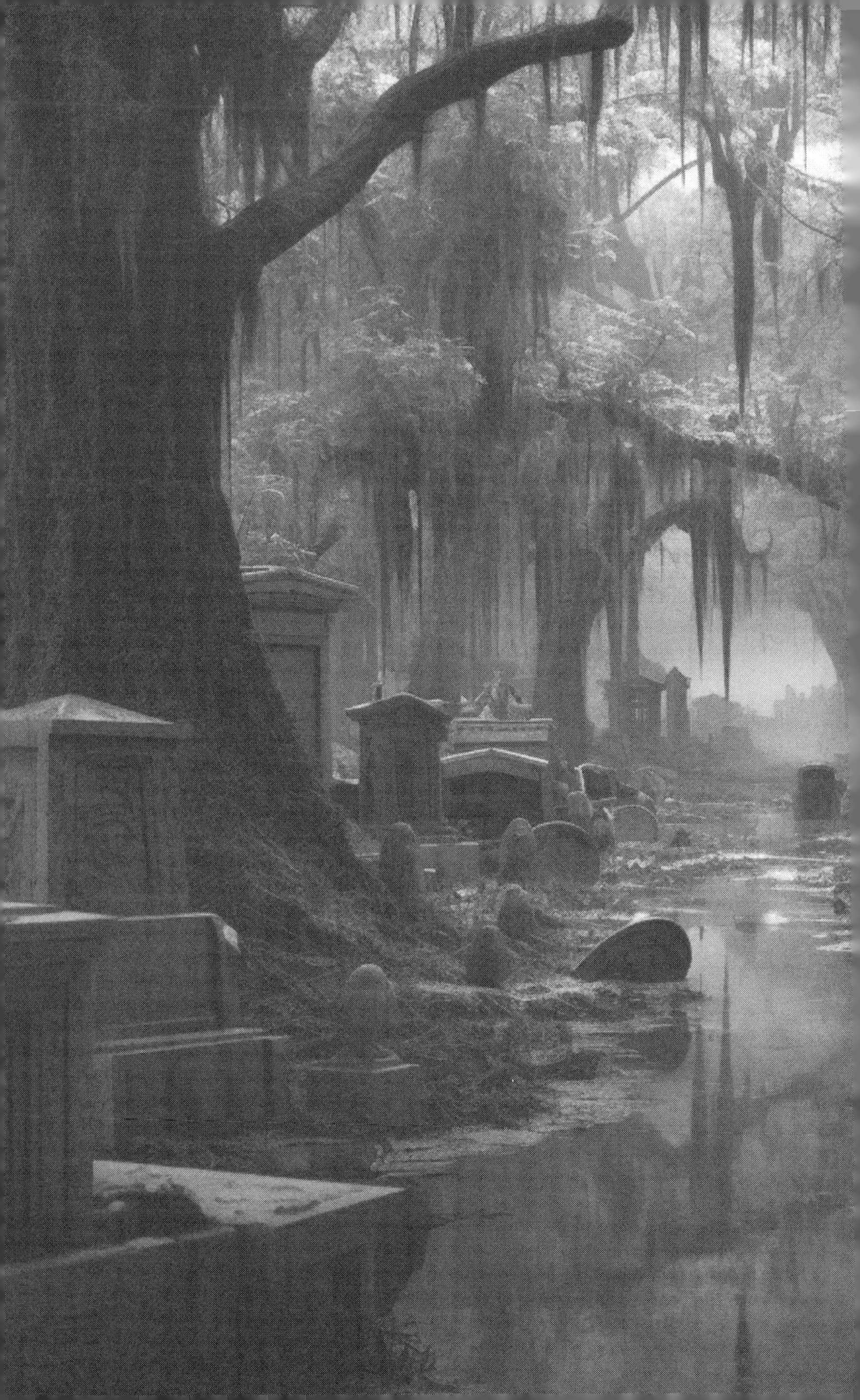

Chapter Eighteen
Hope for the Future

Three Days Later

The morning sunlight filtered through the curtains, bathing the bedroom in a warm glow as Hazel reluctantly slid her feet out of bed and onto the hardwood floor. The scent of freshly brewed coffee and sizzling bacon wafted from the kitchen, beckoning her to follow. She padded down out of the master suite, her exhaustion momentarily forgotten at the prospect of a hearty breakfast.

"Good morning, sleepyhead," Tate called out as she entered the kitchen. He stood by the stove, flipping pancakes with a bright smile on his face, his dark hair still tousled from sleep. It was a look that always made her knees weak. "You look like you could use some coffee."

"Thanks." Crossing the room, she slid into his arms, closing her eyes as he hugged her tight and kissed her forehead. When she backed away, he handed her a mug of coffee. "It smells delicious."

Tate pressed one more kiss to her face, this time to her lips, and then gestured toward the table. "Sit down, I'll get everything ready."

When Hazel had settled into her seat, he filled their plates with generous servings of pancakes, bacon, and scrambled eggs, setting them down on the table. "Bon appétit!"

Candy and Jake appeared in the kitchen a moment later, lowering themselves into the empty chairs. Although they couldn't eat, they still liked to sit at the table as a family. "Morning, doll. How'd you sleep?"

Taking another sip of her coffee, Hazel smiled. "Really well actually. Knowing Bella is doing okay has certainly released some of the tension I've been holding. Now, if only the two of you could have sex a little bit quieter."

Tate stifled a laugh, nearly spitting his coffee across the table.

Candy rolled her eyes. "Like the two of you have any room to talk. The only way to drown it out is to moan louder."

Unable to help herself, Hazel laughed and repeated Candy's response to Tate, who laughed again. "She's not lying. This is the one moment I'm glad I can't hear them."

Their banter was interrupted by the shrill ring of Hazel's cellphone. Hazel's heart skipped a beat as she rose to answer it, her mind automatically going to the worse case scenario. Instead, she was greeted by the familiar voice of her mother.

"Good morning, sweetheart. I told you I would call you when your father is awake and able to talk to you."

Returning to the table, Hazel put her phone on loudspeaker, a mix of emotions bubbling within her. "That's great to hear, Mom." She glanced at Tate, who had paused mid-bite to listen. "Tate and I actually have some news to share with you both."

"News?" her mother echoed, curiosity clear in her voice. "Well let me get your father on the call too."

The beeping sounds of the hospital became louder as her mother placed the phone closer to her father, turning on the loudspeaker.

"Hi, Dad," she said, trying to keep her voice steady. "I'm sorry I'm not there to see you in the hospital."

"Hello, my girl," her father replied, his voice hoarse from days of being intubated.

Hazel took a deep breath, anxiety twisting her stomach. "Tate and I are expecting a baby."

"Really? Oh, honey, that's wonderful news!" her mother exclaimed, joy dripping from her voice. Hazel could picture the wide smile on Sandi's face, and it brought warmth to her own heart.

"Congratulations to you both," her father added, clearing his throat. "I'm so happy for the two of you."

Reaching across the table, Tate took her hand, lifting it to his lips and kissing it.

"Thanks, Mom...Dad." Tears pricked at the corners of her eyes. "We're really happy."

Two Weeks Later

Hazel and Tate met Bella and her father at an ice cream shop near her home, the little girl's face lighting up when she spotted them. With their frozen treats in hand, Hazel went straight to the table, lowering herself to the floor and giving Bella a big hug.

"Thank you for inviting us," Bella's father said, his warm gaze resting on Hazel. "It's all Bella has been talking about since she woke up in the hospital."

"We're glad to have you both here," Tate replied, setting their ice cream down on the table. For once, Hazel felt like everything was falling into place—family, friends, and love all fitting perfectly together like the layers of a banana split.

Taking a seat next to the little girl who'd been haunting her dreams for months, Hazel listened as Bella rambled on about all the new toys she got when she was in the hospital and how excited she was to return to school. To Hazel's relief, Bella looked healthy. Her hair was in pigtails, the orange ribbons matching her Halloween-themed dress. Hazel's gaze shifted from Bella's sparkling eyes to the melting ice cream in front of them, shoving a spoonful of cookies and cream into her mouth and relishing the taste as it balanced her emotions. The sweetness acted as a reminder that amidst the chaos, there were still moments worth savoring.

"Your powers," Bella said, her tiny voice hesitant. "You've been able to control them for a while now, right?"

Although Hazel wasn't sure she wanted to talk about it in a public place, she nodded. "Yes. I mean, sometimes they're a bit unpredictable...because they change...but I can control them for the most part."

"Would you be willing to help me?" Bella asked, her eyes lighting up. "I don't know much about my own abilities, and I think I could learn a lot from you."

Before responding, Hazel glanced at the little girl's father, who had paused in his chat with Tate to listen. "I'd love to mentor you...but...um...only if your dad says it's okay."

He smiled at the two of them. "As long as it doesn't interfere with her schoolwork, I think it's a wonderful idea. The more my baby girl learns about her powers, the better she can protect herself."

"Thank you, Daddy." Dropping her spoon, Bella wrapped her arms around her father, giving him a big kiss on the cheek. The show of affection warmed Hazel's chest. With the little girl having lost her mother in such a traumatic way, Hazel was just glad Bella still had a parent who loved her.

With their ice cream date finished, Tate led Hazel outside, grabbing her hand and giving it a gentle squeeze. "I have one more surprise for you."

"Another surprise?" Hazel raised an eyebrow, curiosity piqued. "What is it?"

Grinning, Tate guided her toward the car. "You'll see."

As they drove through the city, the sun dipped below the horizon, casting a golden hue over the buildings. Hazel felt her anticipation rise with every turn they took, wondering what Tate had planned.

When their destination came into view, a rooftop restaurant she'd always wanted to go to, and Tate pulled up to the valet, her heart melted. "Are you serious? A surprise date night?"

"Anything to see that smile on your face," he replied, helping her out of the car and leading her to the elevator.

Hazel's chest swelled with love as she sat down at the reserved table that offered a breathtaking view of the cityscape. Even amid the turmoil and uncertainty that surrounded them, his unwavering support meant the world to her.

"Thank you." Sliding her hand around his neck, she pulled him close, pressing her lips to his. "This is perfect."

Tate's love was undeniable as he gazed into her eyes, sliding his hand up to cup her cheek. "Anything for you."

As they talked and laughed over their romantic dinner, the burdens of the past few days seemed to lift, replacing them with love and hope for the future. No matter what challenges lay ahead, Hazel knew they would face them as one, their love an unstoppable force guiding them through the darkness.

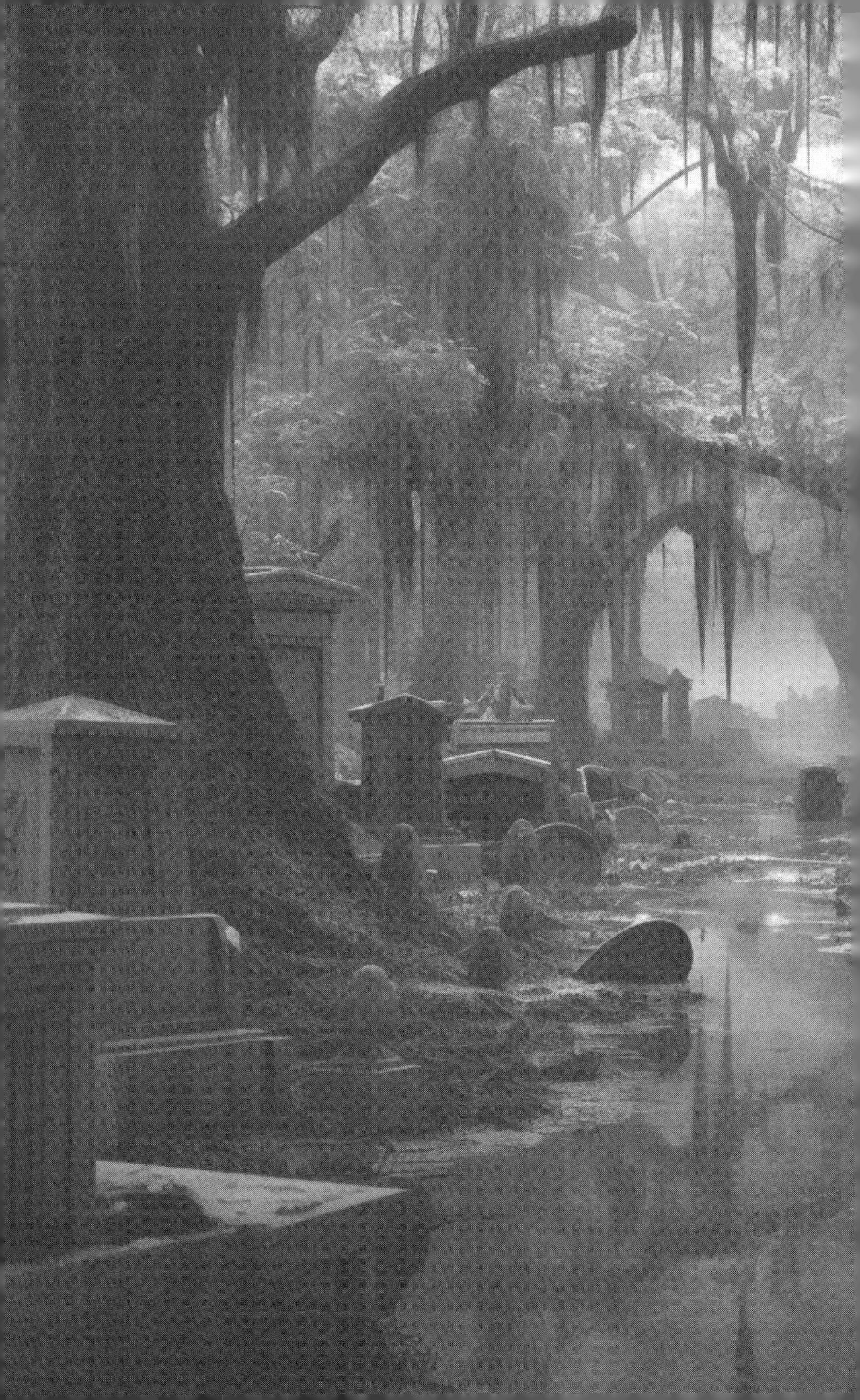

Epilogue

The Darkness that Follows

The moonlight filtered through the thin curtains, projecting a silvery glow upon Tate's sleeping form as Hazel lay nuzzled against his chest. She closed her eyes, allowing unconsciousness to drift in and take her.

Drifting deeper into sleep, her subconscious mind explored the ethereal landscape of her dreams. Images and sounds merged in a symphony of colors, creating an emotional tapestry that would take her a long time to unravel once awake.

As Hazel's dream world morphed and twisted, vibrant hues melted into each other, like watercolors bleeding together. The cacophony of memories and emotions settled, leaving behind a dimly lit chamber with tall stone walls covered in creeping ivy. Hazel stood in the middle of the room, barefoot on a cold stone floor, her arms wrapped around her center.

"Hello?" she called out, her voice echoing in the cavernous room.

As if made of wisps of fog, a figure emerged from the shadows, its form almost translucent. The desperation in the spirit's wide eyes opened a gaping pit in her stomach.

"I'm here to warn you, Hazel," the spirit whispered, its voice straining. "There is danger lurking in the shadows, waiting to ensnare you."

Hazel's brow furrowed as she tried to make sense of the spirit's words. "What danger? Who are you?"

"I cannot linger long." The spirit's outline flickered as it struggled to maintain its presence. "Trust your instincts and be vigilant. The darkness that follows you threatens to consume everything you treasure."

With each word, the spirit's desperation grew more palpable, fear seeping into the very air around them and finding its way through Hazel's skin. The gravity of the situation pressed down on her chest, making it difficult to breathe. "What do you mean? What darkness?" Hazel's heart raced as she tried to process the warning, her mind reeling with questions. "Why me? What do I need to do?"

"Trust yourself," the spirit whispered, reaching out a trembling hand to Hazel. "Only you can stop this darkness."

As the spirit disappeared, the chamber around Hazel crumbled, the once-solid walls dissolving into dust. The urgency of the spirit's warning echoed in her ears, its fear now hers.

As a sinister whisper echoed through the crumbling chamber, Hazel's dream's atmosphere shifted and became heavy and oppressive. Shadows slithered across the edge of her vision, closing in like vipers.

"Don't forget...trust yourself," the spirit's voice echoed, but it was faint and distorted, as if carried by the wind.

The shadows encroached further, and an inexplicable sensation of dread tightened around Hazel's heart, threatening to suffocate her. Her body trembled from the cold, but more so from the unease set deep within her.

The remnants of the dream lingered in Hazel's mind as she clutched her sweat-drenched sheets, her breathing labored. The spirit's warning was still ringing in her ears, and she struggled to understand the messages she'd received as she sat up in bed. She glanced around her room, seeking comfort in the familiar surroundings, but even Tate's warmth beside her could not relieve her fear.

Her breath slowed and her nerves calmed as she laid back down, but she couldn't help but feel like the spirit's warning wasn't a figment of her imagination. Even though she did not know what its warning meant for her, she knew that she needed to stay vigilant, trust her instincts, and face the darkness that lay ahead.

"Two scoops," she whispered into the night, her voice trembling. "I'll need more than two scoops to face this."

To be continued.

Enjoyed The Spirit Collector?

If you enjoyed The Spirit Collector, please leave a review! I really appreciate it!

https://books2read.com/u/4EpEYA

Also By C.A. Varian

Hazel Watson Mystery Series
Kindred Spirits: Prequel
The Sapphire Necklace
Justice for the Slain
Whispers from the Swamp
Crossroads of Death
The Spirit Collector

Crown of the Phoenix Series
Crown of the Phoenix
Crown of the Exiled
Crown of the Prophecy (Coming Soon)
Mate of the Phoenix

Supernatural Savior Series
Song of Death
Goddess of Death

An Other World Series
The Other World

The Other Key
The Other Fate (coming January 2024)

My Alien Mate Series
My Alien Protector

Saving Scarlett (coming January 2024)

Second Chance with Santa (Coming December 2023)

Follow C.A. Varian

Sign up for C. A. Varian's newsletter to receive current updates on her new and upcoming releases, sales, and giveaways:

You can also find all stories, books, and social media pages and follow her here:

https://linktr.ee/cavarian

https://cavarian.com/

About the Author

Raised in a small town in the heart of Louisiana's Cajun Country, C. A. Varian spent most of her childhood fishing, crabbing, and getting sunburnt at the beach. Her love of reading began very young, and she would often compete at school to read enough books to earn prizes.

Graduating with the first of her college degrees as a mother of two in her late twenties, she became a public-school teacher. As of the release of this book, she was finally able to resign from teaching to write full time!

Writing became a passion project, and she put out her first novel in 2021, and has continued to publish new novels every few months since then, not slowing down for even a minute.

Married to a retired military officer, she spent many years moving around for his career, but they now live in central Alabama, with her youngest daughter, Arianna. Her oldest daughter, Brianna, is enjoying her happily ever after with her new husband and several pups. C. A. Varian has two Shih Tzus that she considers her children. Boy, Charlie, and girl, Luna, are their mommy's shadows. She also has three cats named Ramses, Simba, and Cookie.

Made in the USA
Columbia, SC
07 January 2025

2777f51c-1b56-44fc-8b5e-19f8770c4e0aR01